Deadly Pattern

Douglas Clark

© Douglas Clark 1970

Douglas Clark has asserted his rights under the Copyright, Design and Patents Act, 1988, to be identified as the author of this work.

First published in 1970 by Cassell & Company Ltd.

This edition published in 2018 by Endeavour Media Ltd.

For Roderick

Table of Contents

Chapter One	7
Chapter Two	23
Chapter Three	38
Chapter Four	68
Chapter Five	83
Chapter Six	97
Chapter Seven	121

Chapter One

Detective Sergeant Hill climbed into the front passenger seat of the big Vauxhall. Detective Sergeant Brant was sitting behind the wheel. Hill said: 'Where's his nibs?'

'Over at the station, phoning the Yard.'

'Telling them to get another feather ready for his cap?'

'Maybe. He deserves it. What's today? Friday? We came up here on Monday. Remember what old Willy P. Green said when we set out?'

'That it would be an impossible case to crack.'

'And Masters had it buttoned up by Thursday night. Not bad going even for him.'

The car was standing outside the Goblin Inn at Rooksby-le-Soken. Diagonally across the square, in the one-room police station, Detective Chief Inspector George Masters was reporting the end of the case to Scotland Yard. Announcing his return that morning. By his side stood Detective Inspector Green.

Green said to the local constable, P.C. Crome, 'How about a nice cup of Nescaff to warm us up before we set out? *We've* done *you* proud. How about *you* spoiling *us* for a change?'

Crome said: 'The kettle's boiling. Will the sergeants be coming too, sir?'

'You can nip down and whistle them over. They're outside the pub.'

Crome used Nescafé and Carnation milk from the tin to make the brew. He handed a blue-banded mug and a bowl of sugar to Green. Placed another on the stained chenille table cover in front of Masters, and clattered down the stairs. The cold February nor'easter had returned, bringing with it a hint of rain. The wind tousled his hair as he stood at the entrance to the station. He put two fingers in his mouth, and whistled piercingly. Even the wind couldn't dissipate the sound. Hill in the closed car heard it. He looked up. Crome waved a signalling arm. The car started to crawl across the square.

Green scalded his mouth on the coffee. Put it down. Lit a Kensitas, and then took time to pay attention to Masters. The Chief put his hand over the mouthpiece, half turned to Green and said: 'Prepare for trouble. And hand me one of those sheets of paper, would you?'

Green passed over a small wad of official crested quarto. He said: 'What're they bellyaching about? A murderer committing suicide?' It was a dig at Masters. The evening before, the man responsible for murdering the vicar of Rooksby—knowing Masters was on to him—had killed himself. Masters recognized the jibe for what it was. Ignored it. He and Green didn't get on. A common enough occurrence where an older man is subordinate to a younger.

'I've been asked to hang on,' said Masters.

'Well I hope they hurry up. I've been away from home long enough. I want to get going.'

Crome and the two sergeants clattered up the stairs. As they came through the door the phone crackled. Masters waved an impatient hand, demanding silence. While he listened the three tip-toed over to get their coffee. Masters said 'Sir' occasionally. Made a few notes as he listened. The conversation ended. He still held the phone. 'Another job,' he told Green. 'That was Commander Curtis. Williams is coming on now.' He put the phone back to his ear. Green grimaced. Masters said 'Sir' again and listened intently. The call lasted another three minutes. Then Masters put the receiver back on the cradle and said: 'No rest for the wicked. Who's got an AA book?'

Commander Williams, still a Yard man, but seconded now to the Home Office, was National Co-ordinator of Regional Crime Squads. Appointed to deal with organized crime, his duties sometimes spilled over into other areas. Green knew that if Williams was concerned, the new case could well be long lasting. He said to Hill: 'Get on to H.Q. and tell them to let my missus and yours know we won't be home tonight or for the next week, likely. Tell them to tell her I'll need some clean shirts and I'll phone the address through tonight.'

'Do any of you ever read the newspapers?' asked Masters.

'When do we get time?' Green said.

'Good lord, chief. Not all those women?' said Brant.

Masters nodded.

'What perishing women?'

'We'll discuss it in the car,' Masters replied. 'Route from here, through Boston and Louth to Hawksfleet and Finstoft.'

The car felt its way carefully out of Rooksby and sped north-east. Masters sat back and filled his pipe with Warlock Flake. The rain came more heavily. Brant set the wipers going. The wind whistled past the car, taking the gathered raindrops away in feathery spatters. If anything, in this part of the journey, the land grew flatter. Fen country. Bulb country. Grey. Bending the knee to the dominant wind.

'What about these women?' Green asked.

Masters replied: 'Five, respectable, married women. Middle class. All of an age . . .'

'What age?'

'Late thirties, early forties.'

'What's happened to them?'

'All five disappeared in the last month. Four of them found, dead and buried.'

'No sign of the fifth?'

'Not yet. But she shouldn't be far away. The other four were found about two hundred yards apart, buried in the dunes at Finstoft.'

Green said: 'Mass murder?'

'It looks like it. A lunatic at large.'

'How were they killed?'

'Throttled.'

'Sexually assaulted, I suppose?'

'They're carrying out tests.'

'Which will probably be inconclusive as they're all married women. What about their clothes? Disarranged, removed, anything of that sort?'

'I've no details.'

'Where does Williams come into this?'

'He's *really* doing some co-ordinating this time,' Masters explained. 'Although all these women were found in Finstoft some of them lived in Hawksfleet. Hawksfleet's a municipal borough with its own police force. Finstoft's a county borough. So its coppers are part of the Lindsey force.

'Lindsey?'

'Administrative part of Lincolnshire. Like the Ridings of Yorkshire. Both forces are interested—or should be—but there appears to be a bit of buck passing.'

'Meaning the Hawksfleet people have been looking for them and the Finstoft people've found them, but neither crowd wants the job of taking on the case. I know. We're Joe Soap again. But this time we've got two lots to please.'

'Or neither,' Hill said. 'I mean the National Co-ordinator'll have told them to give us a free hand, won't he?'

Masters said: 'Maybe. We'll assume he has.'

Green said: 'I'll bet neither side has dredged up any leads for us.'

'They haven't.'

'Typical. So how many suspects are there? Thousands?'

'Over a hundred thousand in Hawksfleet and about thirty thousand in Finstoft,' said Masters. 'All jumbled up into one nice, cosy conurbation. "Inextricably linked" was Williams' phrase. He sounded as if he thought it would take some sorting out.'

'I'll bet. On the east coast in a north-east gale. Cosy's about the right word for it.'

The conversation lapsed. The countryside changed. Small rounded hills. The Wolds. Louth with its tall-spired church. Green said: 'A bit different from Boston Stump.' Nobody replied. The air in the car was heavy with smoke. The next signpost said Hawksfleet—13 miles: Finstoft—15 miles. Green said: 'I'm going to have fish for lunch.'

'Hawksfleet or Finstoft, chief?' Brant inquired.

'Finstoft. Where the bodies are there shall we be also.'

Green grunted but made no comment. When they came to the outskirts of Hawksfleet, Hill had to ask the way twice. They arrived at the Finstoft police station just before one o'clock.

Superintendent Bullimore was pleased to see them. He was in uniform. Bulky, but wasp-waisted. His belt split him in two. His face podgy and shapeless, covered in small red veins, from the tip of his purplish nose to the lobes of his ears. The result of long beats in strong cold winds. Little hair; and what there was of it, grey, to match his eyes. His fingers stiff-jointed through living in a hard-water area for too long. He said: 'When the National Co-ordinator rang me to say you were coming I could have sung the Alleluia chorus. I could, straight.' His U's were broad, all alike, with no differing shades. It sounded strange to the southerners. Masters said: 'As bad as that, is it, sir?'

'Bad? We're living in a madhouse here. Five murders all at once and we haven't had one in over twenty years. We need somebody who's more used to killings than we are to sort this lot out, I can tell you. But we won't talk at the moment. What you'll need is a bite of dinner.'

'Please.'

'Well now, you can go straight to your hotel about a mile away, or we can pop up the hill to a pub on the High Street where we can have a drink and a lemon if you like.'

'Lemon?' Green said.

'Aye. Lemon. Fish, lad, fish.'

'Oh.'

'You've never heard of it? Well, you know a plaice when you see one?'

'Yes.'

'Got red spots on. Right? And a sole's got yellow spots. Well a lemon looks like a plaice and has yellow spots. Some say they're half and half—crossbred like. Others just say they have characteristics of both. I don't mind. I like 'em and I eat 'em. Lemons!' His lips-smacked as he said it.

Green said: 'And for me.'

They all five squeezed into the Vauxhall and drove up the hill to the Prawner, sandwiched between a new supermarket and a wear-now-pay-later tailor's. The wind when they got out of the car was still cold, but now had the tang of salt in it. A skin-stinging rain struck them on the cheeks. They were glad to reach the Snug in the Prawner.

*

Back at the station after lunch Bullimore said to Masters: "You'll be wanting our notes to read. What about a verbal briefing?'

'If you could let us have the story. I'd like all four of us to hear it. It'll save passing your paperwork round each one in turn.'

'Good for you. I prefer to hear things straight out myself. Come on in here.' His room had an open fire, and not much more in the way of comfort. The furniture was yellow-varnished. The floor covered in bottle-green linoleum. The uncurtained window looked out on to a small parade ground and a row of lock-up garages. Great slashes of wind-blown rain struck the panes almost horizontally. Masters took an upright chair too small for him and motioned his colleagues to seat themselves.

Bullimore said: 'By heck, you're a big chap. I bet your mam would rather feed you for a week than a fortnight.' Masters didn't reply. He took his pipe from his breast pocket, where he kept it, bowl to the top, wedged upright with a white silk handkerchief. He had opened the brassy tin of Warlock Flake and was rubbing a fill in the palm of his left hand, with the heel of his right, before Bullimore spoke again.

'Five women missing and we've found four of them. Frances Burton, Brenda Pogson, Cynthia Baker and Joanna Osborn—in order of disappearance from their homes. The one we haven't found is Barbara Severn, but she went missing second, after Mrs Burton and before Mrs Pogson.

'Now I'd better tell you that only two of them—Burton and Osborn—are Finstoft women. The others come from Hawksfleet. And in Finstoft we haven't had anybody reported missing—except a few kids who run away from home and are lugged back again pretty quick—for over six years. In Hawksfleet they have a few more go off untraced because . . . well, they're a port, and they get quite a lot of young lasses hanging round the docks. Sailors and fishermen coming ashore with pay to spend are easy pickings. And every now and again one of these girls disappears. But even Hawksfleet doesn't get respectable married women going off unbeknown to anybody. Leastways not in groups of three at a time.'

Masters said: 'So before you found any of their bodies you were interested in these women—as missing persons?'

'That's right. Mrs Burton was last seen on the evening of January the tenth. Her husband didn't report to us until the twelfth. Said he thought she'd gone off without warning him to see her mother and he didn't want to make a fuss by bringing us in. We did the usual—hospitals and railway stations, circulated descriptions etcetera, etcetera, to try and trace her. Then about three days later the Hawksfleet people chipped in with Mrs Severn—her we haven't found yet.'

'That would be the fifteenth of January. But at that time you still didn't suspect murder?'

'No reason to. It looked like a bit of a coincidence, but there was only one in each borough. It was when Hawksfleet got to hear about Mrs Pogson on the nineteenth and Mrs Baker on the twenty-fifth that they started to sit up and take notice. Our last one, Mrs Osborn, was on the twenty-eighth.'

'You then began to treat the disappearances as murder?'

'We did. But we'd nothing to go on. No sign where any of them were. Until this Tuesday. There's a chap called Tolley. Has a little dog. He walks it along the front here in all weathers. We all know him. Bit of a character. Used to be a window cleaner. On Tuesday he was out along the dunes, past the end of the town and beyond the embankment. When there's an easterly wind and spring tides you never know what's going to be washed up in the dunes. Anything from an old cod's-liver barrel to a transistor radio. And if you happen to have the time, and an old sack to sling over your back, and a terrier dog that's been taught to nose things out—well, who knows what you might not find.'

'And Tolley's dog found—now let me see—which one did he find? Not necessarily the one that disappeared first,' said Masters.

Bullimore replied: 'I can see you've got all your buttons sewn on. Mrs Baker it was. And she'd been number four to go missing. She'd been buried close to the water's edge—just above normal high water mark. But when you've got a high wind with the springs the water comes in further. Right up the beach to the dunes behind and sometimes further than that. Last week-end's gales and high seas uncovered the body—or some of it. The dog found a bit of rag sticking out of the sand. He was worrying it when Tolley reached him. Tolley called him off, but he wouldn't leave what he'd got, so Tolley went to investigate. He thought it might be something worth digging out because the terrier didn't often make mistakes.'

'And that's how Mrs Baker was found?'

'Aye. The Hawksfleet people identified her, and we decided that if five women with a lot in common had all gone missing at about the same time, and we'd found one of them, it was likely we'd find the others. We prodded the rest of the beach first, with long spikes, but we had no joy. Then the tide came in again and so we started prodding among the dunes. By Wednesday night, besides Mrs Baker, we'd got Mrs Osborn, Mrs Burton and Mrs Pogson, in that order. We're still trying to find Mrs Severn.'

Master said: 'So far all the bodies have been found in your area, but they're a mixture of Hawksfleet and Finstoft women. Were you a bit undecided as to which one of you should carry out the investigation?'

'Not really. I knew they were my responsibility, but it seems likely half the work will have to be done in Hawksfleet. That means a lot of liaison both ways, so we decided it would be better if a third party were called in, who'd have experience of this sort of thing which we haven't got, and who'd not be afraid to step over the boundary from one patch to the other.'

'So you asked the Yard for help.'

'No. I asked 'em for *you*. Yesterday. They said I couldn't have you as you were on that murdered parson case. Then today I was told you'd be here by one o'clock.'

'Our business in Rooksby finished sooner than we expected.'

'So I heard. Now you've got a lunatic to catch. And the sooner the better. Since the news got out on Tuesday nobody's dared go on the streets after dark. It makes it better for us, but it's a bad thing really.'

'I'm sure it is.' Masters got up and stretched his legs. 'Your notes will tell us what you've done so far.'

Bullimore slapped the file on his desk. 'It's all here. Hawksfleet's reports as well as ours.'

'Good. But before we start, I want to know about this area. I've never been here before. Give me a potted history. What sort of people are they?'

'Is that how you go about it?' asked Bullimore.

'I find it helps if I know the type of people I'm working among.'

'I've told him before, Super,' said Green. 'Everybody's alike if you take a cross section. But he won't have it. He's one of these moderns. Psychology of crime.'

Bullimore said a little tartly: 'If that's what he wants he can have it. It brings home the bacon, doesn't it?'

'Sometimes,' Masters said modestly.

'More often than not from what I've heard. So here goes. We're what you'd call an isolated community here. You've only got to look at a map to see it. We can't move north because of the Humber. We can't move east because of the North Sea. That leaves us two directions—south and west. And even so you've got to go a hell of a way before you get anywhere.

'Before the war the only people who wandered our way were trippers and visitors from Sheffield and Leeds who came to see t'watter as they called it.'

'Is it different now?' Masters asked.

'Very. In some ways. You'd know more about the effects of migration on culture and such-like stuff than I do. But what I can say is that we'd very little except home-grown culture here. And I'll tell you why. Hawksfleet started making money from trawling in the First World War. Selling fish to the services made rich men of quite a few who would have been on the bread-line else.'

'Why?' said Green.

'Because you couldn't fish in a big enough way in the days before ice-making to make a lot of money. Then when the war came you could bring anything ashore and sell it in any state you liked to a ready-made market. That's when this place started to boom. Of course some of the owners and lads who should have benefited didn't. The owners who gave all their ships for minesweeping and the fishermen who manned them got nowt out of it but a chance of being blown up and drowned. But money came in, and it started dividing the community up into what-d'you-call-its—levels . . .?'

'Strata?'

'That's the word. Financial strata. Some pretty plumb ignorant people found themselves on the top of the pyramid. And you know what happens then? They're the biggest bloody snobs you can get. And what happens at the top works its way down. Every level of income was too good for the one below it. Talk about caste system! It was pathetic. And there was nobody to bust it wide open. Nobody came and went. Those who were here—well, the better-britched ones—were sitting pretty, and the others couldn't afford to go. And like I said, there wasn't much culture. Some tried to get a bit. Those who could afford it. But it wasn't easy for anybody who hadn't the brass to belong to clubs and societies and to travel.'

'The last war changed it all?'

'You'd never believe it. We're pretty exposed here, you know. Straight opposite trouble as you might say. So we got a big influx of troops. And of course Hawksfleet was a station, not only for the minesweepers, but for the navy and freighters too. And our own lads and lasses were called up and went away all over the world. That began it. They didn't let things settle back to what they had been when they came home. And of course there's more cars and travel now than there was, so we're not cut off quite as much. So we've levelled out a bit. You haven't got the divisions you once had.'

'But there are remnants of class-consciousness.'

Bullimore lit a cigarette and twirled the match into the fire. 'Aye. Remnants. Not so much among the youngsters, but from about forty upwards they're still fighting to hang on. From forty to about fifty-five they're not too bad because they got a bit better education than their parents. There's an old saying in Finstoft that you could only make money round here in the old days if you could manage to put two aitches in piano. If you'd got a degree all you'd get was a job as a draft clerk. Opening and closing windows.'

'You're not pulling your punches,' said Masters.

'I'm not. I've seen grown men and children insulted and hurt for no reason other than the fact that they couldn't afford to dress as well as some others. And by the same token I've seen some fawned on as couldn't hold a candle to a good dustman. I don't know which I've thought the worst of. Those who did the fawning or the ones on the receiving end.'

'It makes you sick to think about it,' said Green. 'If these women were the sort who stuck their noses in the air, they deserved what they got.'

'I'm not saying *they* did. But their dads and mams did, you can bet your life. They're all in about the same income group now; and they came from the same sort. Like married like round here until a few years back.'

'Thank you,' said Masters. 'It's been an enlightening discussion. We'll at least know we've to wear our best caste marks, and we'll be on the lookout for untouchables, pariahs and the like.'

Bullimore looked at him suspiciously, but Masters proceeded quietly to relight his pipe. Outside the rain was still slashing down and the wind had started to moan. Suddenly a long blast found a crack round the window frame and came in noisily, rattling the venetian blind like a Gatling-gun going full lick. Hill said: 'Are they still looking for the fifth body, sir?'

'In this? Be your age, sergeant.' Hill blushed. Bullimore softened his tone. 'No, lad. When the wind starts to moan like that you'll know it's come in with the tide, And the beach out there'll be under water, and the dunes most likely.' He grinned suddenly and turned to Masters. 'Besides, there's no use in having a dog and barking yourself. Now you're here we'll leave you to it.'

Masters stopped opposite to him and looked down at him. 'That's what we want—normally. But just to begin with I'd like a bit of help.'

'What sort? C.I.D.?'

'No. A man to act as a guide mostly. I don't want to have to waste my time looking for houses and places in Hawksfleet and Finstoft. Haven't you got some old P.C. who knows the place like the back of his hand who'll be glad to gossip to us?'

Bullimore sat back in his chair, his head sunk in his collar. 'Old P.C.? I've got one that's just recovering from flu and's due to retire at the end of April. He's a bit slow on his feet and in the head, but he's a right old Tofter. Been here since he was born and never been out of the place as far as I can make out. If you'll see he keeps wrapped up so's we don't have to pay him a disability increment to his pension for the rest of his natural, I'll see if I can let you have him. If you're sure you wouldn't rather have one of the so-called bright young 'uns.'

'I've got plenty of those. I'll take the old boy. What's his name?'

'Garner. Fred Garner. When d'you want him?'

'Tomorrow morning. At our pub at nine.'

'Right. Talking of pubs. There's only one decent one open at this time of the year. The Estuary. It's on the front. I've booked you in and I'll take you there when you're ready to go.'

Masters looked at his watch. 'It's getting on for four, so we'll call it a day. I can't see us doing anything useful outside in this weather and what's left of the daylight.'

Bullimore reached for his cap. Masters went on: 'There's no need for you to turn out. If you've such a thing as a road map of the town. . . .'

Bullimore picked up his internal phone. Shortly afterwards the clerk came in with a road map and a six-inch-to-the-mile plan of the dune area where the bodies had been discovered. Bullimore handed this latter straight over to Masters and pointed out the ink crosses where the women had been buried: each cross marked with a name. 'I had that prepared for you. When you get out there you'll find the places marked well enough on the ground. Now for your hotel. You're here.' Bullimore put a thick forefinger on the map and traced the route from the Police Station. 'Go the same way as we went to the Prawner. Up the hill that was. Turn left along the High Street and right when you come to the T-junction. After that it's plain sailing. This road runs right along the front, you see, but inside the promenade. There's only houses on one side. That'll be your right. Go on until you come to the floral gardens with the low, hoop-topped railings on your left. You'll see shelters in the gardens. When you get to the second one you'll see the Estuary just ahead on your right. It's bang on the road, but there's a car park at the back.'

Masters folded the map. 'Thanks. We'll be off then. I'll keep in touch, but I hope you'll attend to the inquests. All I'll want to know is the verdict.'

'It's all laid on. Not until Monday.'

'And we'll want to know if they were sexually assaulted. Might as well know the type we're looking for,' added Green.

Bullimore got to his feet ponderously, and rubbed one forefinger round the inside of his already overtight collar. Masters, watching him, was amused to see he appeared slightly embarrassed by the question. Finally he said: 'I think the doctor'd better tell you. He's been working on it and he's got some fantouche theory that you'll want to speak to him about. I'll tell you what. I'll ask him to contact you at the Estuary tonight—if that's all right with you.'

Masters said: 'Ideal. I'd rather he didn't phone. D'you think he'd mind calling?'

'If I know Eric Swaine he'll come if there's the ghost of a chance of being offered a Taddy Strong Ale.'

'He's a soak?' asked Green.

Bullimore grinned. 'Well, now, you're asking me. I'd have said that anybody else who took what he does would be an alcoholic, but he's never affected by it. He's got some theory about that, too. He had ulcers or something and had half his stomach removed. He reckons that you take in alcohol through the stomach, and as he's only got half a one he only soaks up half of what he drinks. How true it all is I don't know, but it seems to work in his case.'

Green stared in disbelief but said nothing. Masters took his coat from the row of pegs on the wall. 'Tell him he shall have his whatever-it-is strong ale if he's *got* to have an inducement. Try and get him to make it about nine. That'll give me a chance to read your reports and have dinner before he comes.'

*

Although it was still an hour before sunset as they set off for the hotel, the daylight was going. Brant was driving. Masters sat behind him with the map on his knees. As they passed along the High Street and came to the T-junction he said: 'Turn right.'

'And straight ahead,' said Brant.

'No. We'll take a different route. Just here. Turn left now.'

Brant obeyed. The car was running down a short, wide road straight for the sea. Green said: 'Just look at those bloody waves.'

'Right,' said Masters. He spoke up to make his voice heard above the screaming of the wind. As Brant turned the car on to the exposed roadway running alongside and level with the promenade at this point a blanket of spray curled over the sea wall and carried on to the car. The heavy drops thudded on the roof. The nearside windows and windscreen were covered in a dirty green, cascading film.

Green flinched. 'We'll be drowned along here.'

'Not us,' said Masters and touched Brant on the shoulder. 'That sign says the speed limit's eight miles an hour along here.'

The heavy car, side on to the wind, rocked as it went. Water swirled over the roadway. Brant used the crown to avoid the worst of it. Nothing was coming the other way. Ahead of them the spray leapt high and broke into big white gobbets of water, like fiery rain crackers on bonfire night. Signboards outside ice-cream kiosks shut for the winter swung frenziedly on their hooks. And all the time the rain came down. It poured from the felted roofs of shuttered shops in inverted, twisted triangular sheets that sometimes fell straight for a moment and were then whirled away in mid-air by the gusts. Masters rubbed his hands. He couldn't decide whether it was because he felt cold or because he was enjoying himself on two counts. First, his own natural delight at braving the elements in a big, comfortable car; secondly, because he was revelling in Green's obvious dislike of the situation.

Green was muttering. Hill had turned up his collar as if to give himself extra protection, but Masters noted he was interested. The estuary, seven miles wide at this point, a heaving mass of grey-brown, murky, viscid matter, blending with a smoked glass horizon, had a fascination. A hundred yards out the swell would break into an almost continuous white line, thin as a cable at first, but lifting and creaming as it swept in to meet the concrete with a slap of gargantuan force.

The road jinked, turned away slightly from the promenade. Floral gardens nosed in between the two. The evergreen bushes dripped. The soil in the beds looked soggy and flattened. The grass crouched, turning its back on the wind. An unlit shelter of wood and glass—four open-fronted boxes under a roof of mock tiles—came into view, just discernible against the grey-green backcloth. Four seats, of long slats on cast-iron frames, painted rural green, and intended for the comfort of those taking the sun and air, added glumness to depression. A few lighted shop windows on the landward side threw cloaks of light across the puddles. The street lamps, their rays refracted by rain, twinkled. A double-decker bus, empty of passengers, splashed towards them, taking more than its fair share of the road. Finstoft appeared dead. Dead from exposure to biting wind and rain. Green said: 'Give me Torquay any day. They've got palm trees there.'

Almost without them realizing it, they drew abreast of the Estuary. Flat-fronted, it gave the impression of leaning into the wind. Masters thought it needed a portico and area railings to give it an appearance of having a solid footing. Brant drew the car up. No doorman or porter ventured across the pavement to meet them. Masters shouldered his way through a swing screen door that the wind was keeping open permanently a few inches. The inner door was opened by a porter. Masters said rather brusquely: 'Bags for four outside. And tell the driver where to park the car, please.' He wanted to see the doorman go out. He felt that at least a gesture should have been made to greet them. He turned to the reception desk on the right. A girl in a black dress with a gold lamé belt, and peroxided hair piled up like a cottage loaf, got up from a small table and sauntered the pace or two towards him. She was not interested. Without looking at him, she drawled: 'Yes?'

'No!'

This brought him her attention. At least this time she said: 'What?' and looked perplexedly at him.

He said: 'I'm Chief Inspector Masters. Superintendent Bullimore has booked four single rooms in my name. Could we have them, please?'

He turned round. Green was with him. Hill and Brant were helping the porter. The receptionist was consulting a booking list. She said: 'Oh, yes. Sign in, please. And how long will you be staying for?'

Green said: 'No longer than we can help.' He picked up a chained biro and signed in. The girl opened her eyes when she saw the address given as Scotland Yard. She said: 'Have you come about the murders?'

'No,' Green said. 'To inspect the drains. Now, where's my key?'

Their attitude seemed to have galvanized the Estuary into some sort of life. A manager appeared and offered afternoon tea in the lounge. Masters said they would forgather for it in ten minutes.

*

As they sat over tea in a corner of the lounge, well out of earshot of the few others who were sharing it with them, Green said: 'It's going to be a bastard. Who's for the beach in this weather?' He opened a sandwich to look at the filling. Evidently decided that anchovied egg would be to his taste and went on: 'From what the Super said we've got nothing more than a list of names and dates to go on. They don't spark very fast in these parts, do they?'

'Five women murdered's going some, I'd have thought,' Hill said. 'I'd call it sparking hard and fast.'

'You would. But they haven't thought up the names of any nutcases to suggest, have they? We're strangers here, but we'll be expected to sort 'em out in no time. Make yourself useful and pour me a cup more tea.'

Masters said evenly: 'And I'll have another, please.' He passed the cup across: 'One line of investigation leaps instantly to mind.'

'That's what I think,' agreed Brant. 'It could be one of the husbands of the dead women. We'll have to consider it.'

Masters nodded and thanked Hill for the tea. 'That's what I meant.'

'Unlikely. What would one chap who wants to get rid of his missus go and strangle four more for?' Green asked.

'Camouflage. Murder two, knock off the real victim, and then murder two more,' explained Brant.

Green said: 'And provide yourself with five alibis? You've got to be good to do it.'

'No, you haven't,' said Brant. 'If you bury the bodies so that they're not found for weeks, who's to say exactly when they were bumped off—to within hours of the actual time? Alibis don't come into it.'

Green took another sandwich and said: 'I don't believe it. I've never come across anybody who's got any sense doing in more than one victim.'

Masters took out his tin of Warlock Flake. The black, trade mark sphinx stood out against the brassy background. He contemplated it for a moment, then looked up. He said: 'I agree with you both. But there are two points to be settled empirically. First, has the murderer of five women—or any murderer, if it comes to that—got any sense, as Inspector Green puts it? Second, would we be justified in ignoring the obvious, just because it is obvious? On the traditional grounds that in any murder the investigator must look closely at the victim's next of kin, we've got to put all five husbands through the hoop. It's the natural—and obvious—starting point.'

'Which,' said Green, trying to use a cake fork on a meringue, 'is exactly what the local bobbies will have done. It'll be in their case notes.'

'But will they have done it to our satisfaction?' Masters said. 'No matter how well they've done their job will we be happy not to cover the same ground? I know that unless we do these things for ourselves I always have a faint niggle at the back of my mind: an uneasy feeling that maybe *we* would have got just some little extra fact that would make all the difference.'

Green had given up the unequal struggle with the cake fork and had wisely picked up the meringue. There were faint traces of cream and sugar round his mouth which he wiped away with the back of his hand before saying: 'It's not that I don't trust local bobbies. It's their notes. They can't put everything in. And it's always the important bits they miss out.'

Masters made no comment on this *volte-face*, but it wasn't lost on Hill and Brant. Hill said: 'I suppose we're lucky it's the weekend. All these characters should be at home when we call.'

'If the weather lets up, we've got to visit the burial ground tomorrow morning. Have we got gum boots?'

Hill nodded. 'Two pairs. None to fit you, though.'

Masters got to his feet. 'Then you'll have to carry me across the dunes.' Before they could reply he went on. 'Come to my room at seven o'clock. We'll have earned a drink by then. So somebody had better do a recce of the bars in this chalet as soon as they take the shutters down.'

Chapter Two

Masters kept them for ten minutes. 'I've read their files,' he said. 'There's a lot in them, but it's uncoordinated, so we'll consider we're starting from scratch.' He spread out the large scale map of the dune area. 'See this?'

Green said: 'It's a village. Huts all over the place.'

'Bungalows,' said Masters. 'Summer bungalows. Hundreds of them. Some laid out in rows. Others all higgledy-piggledy, but each with its piece of garden.'

'So what?'

'They'll have been empty in the winter. Nobody to question about mysterious goings on in the dunes. Our friend'll have had a free hand.'

'Did the locals say whether any of the bungalows had been broken into?' Brant asked.

Masters looked down his nose. 'What d'you expect in this day and age? Into the teens have been forced open since last autumn when they were locked up for the winter.'

Green said: 'So there's been a lot of stuff pinched.'

'Surprisingly little. Evidently the owners have learned their lesson by now. About the only things they leave are iron-framed bedsteads. The rest goes home for the winter.'

They bent over the map. Green said: 'These crosses, marking the graves. All except Mrs Baker's, which is on the foreshore, are dotted about among the bungalows. Were any of the ones near the graves broken open?'

Masters shook his head. 'I'd thought of that. As far as I can tell nothing matches. Of course the graves are a long way apart, and there are two break-ins within the triangle formed by the bodies of Osborn, Burton and Pogson. But plotting them on the map doesn't seem to suggest anything to me.'

'It might,' said Hill, 'after we've seen the area itself.'

Masters tapped out his pipe. 'Take a tape, protractor and compass with us tomorrow. We'll measure up, to see that the graves are correctly plotted and not just map-spotted. Now, if we're all ready, what about that drink?'

'Take your choice,' said Green. 'There's an American bar with a pansy behind it serving crème de menthe to a couple of old women, or the Sundowner bar in the basement that looks like a pub and has a barmaid who looks like a barmaid to go with it.'

Masters opted for the Sundowner.

What had been a cellar, approached by a very narrow flight of new, light oak stairs, had been panelled throughout in mock linenfold. There was no window in the room, but the effect was pleasing. The atmosphere was warm and air conditioned. The tables were limed oak and the chairs and wall benches had red seats. The bar was well stocked and, as Masters was pleased to see, had several batteries of beer pumps. There were four people present when they entered. A man sitting alone, on a stool, at the far end of the bar, drinking either gin or vodka, and a middle-aged couple sitting on the bench in a corner. The fourth, the barmaid, was—as Green had said—typical. She was busty, with hair too gold to be true. Her black frock was tight and cut low enough to show the beginnings of emphasized cleavage. Her face was heavily powdered over pleasant, rounded features, the skin of which was coarsened by an over-liberal use of poor cosmetics in the past. On her left hand she had wedding and engagement rings. On the right a stone of indeterminate type, mottled green and big as a glass alley. She was leaning against the jutting main shelf of a Welsh dresser-type cabinet behind her. The metal foil cork covers of several small bottles had been opened out, and stood in a rank behind her head, giving the impression of a tiara of golden fan shells. She came forward as they approached. Masters thought her perfume reminded him of stale currant buns. She said 'Good evening' pleasantly enough in a gin and fags voice and waited for them to name their individual poisons.

Masters turned to the man at the end of the bar. He said 'Good evening' and getting no response except a brief glance, directed his attention back to his own drink.

Green said: 'Quiet this evening, Mrs . . . er . . .?'

'Shirley Moffat. Known as Shirl, love. And we're always a bit quiet on Fridays about now. All the commercials have gone for the weekend, you see. And who'd want to come out on a night like this? It's not fit to send a fiddler's bitch out in, if you'll pardon the expression.'

'I'll pardon it all right. If you'll tell me why a fiddler's bitch.'

'They're the ones that always get drunk, aren't they?'

'I see. So everybody in here's resident?'

'Everybody, including you.'

The conversation lapsed. The man at the end of the bar ordered another drink. He *was* on gin. With water. Masters shuddered mentally. It was a taste he loathed. He wondered what sort of a character this man was, toping gin and water alone in Finstoft on a Friday night in mid-February. His feet on the rung of the stool, hooked in by the heels, were in black pre-polished Chelsea boots. The suit a dark one, with a faint hint of reddish-purple about it, the shirt well-cut round the neck, reminding Masters very much of the Golden Rapides he always wore himself. The tie a nondescript blue, with what looked like a tier of three white sabres just below the knot. The hands were big but fine, with pronounced joints and strangely bold veins. They appeared never to be still—twirling the glass or tracing a pattern on the side of it. The dark hair was thinning, but not flattened. Seen from in front he appeared to have quite a good head still left. Masters guessed that a photograph from above would show the scalp through the thatch. The face was pale, long and narrow, with deep set brown eyes, ringed by an unhealthily dark surround. The beard area was already dark. The ears without lobes lay flat against the head. Masters guessed his height to be little short of six feet, and thought the man looked far from well.

The new drink was placed in front of the stranger. Shirl said: 'Five an' four, Mr Tintern.' Tintern handed over three florins and, when he got it, dropped the eightpence change into a glass ashtray discreetly placed near one of the rows of beer handles. Masters guessed that the two or three sixpences already in it were bait, put there by Shirl herself. He glanced along the bar to prove his theory. Each array of handles had its ashtray with reminder coins. He wondered what Green's comment would be when he realized he was expected to tip this typical barmaid. A movement from Tintern caused Masters to glance at him again. The gin had disappeared and Tintern had already got down from the stool. The empty glass was there. Its contents must have been taken in one swig: coughed back like vodka at a Kremlin banquet. Tintern passed behind them and out of the Sundowner without a word. Green, grasping a half empty pint pot said: 'Matey sort of chap, isn't he? Like a secret drinker. I'm suspicious of secret drinkers.' He lifted his pot and drank noisily.

'There's no need to be suspicious of him,' remarked Hill.

'And why not?' said Brant.

'Because Shirl said we're all residents here. And if he's a resident he's not likely to be local. And if he's not a local he can't be implicated in this job.'

'I suppose not.'

Green said: 'You've decided it is a local then?'

Hill plonked his pot on the bar and nodded. 'All the signs point to it.' He turned to Masters. 'Don't they?'

'We can't afford to be dogmatic, but . . . yes, I must confess I'd say we're looking for a local. A man unfamiliar with the area would be unlikely to sort out five women with such common factors of age and class. But even more important, he would be unlikely to be able to carry out the mechanics of the crime.'

'Mechanics? Throttling them, you mean?' said Green.

'No. Any man with sufficient strength could do that. I'm talking about inveigling what I take to be a bunch of highly respectable women to a place or places where he could murder them. Doesn't it occur to you that these are not Jack the Ripper crimes? Committed at the point of meeting, wherever that may have been? This man has done one of two things in every case. He's managed to attract his victims to the bungalow village in winter, and there killed them. Or he's attracted them to some house or other private spot, killed them there, and then transported the bodies to the bungalow village. We don't know which, but I'd say that in order to do it he'd have to be really well known to each of his victims. That suggests he *is* a local man and, what is more, a man of middle class.'

'Are you sure, chief?' said Brant. 'Couldn't he have jumped them in a quiet spot, bundled them into a car and away?'

'Of course I'm not sure. But I would think your theory more feasible if he'd clobbered them over the head first. But he didn't. He strangled them—and nothing more. No head wounds or bruises. And I don't think that any man could throttle five women in any street this crowd was likely to use, without at least several of them being able to cry out or somebody else noticing the incident.'

Green grunted and put down his empty mug. The clatter on the bar attracted Shirl's attention. She moved down and without a word started to draw the refills. Green said: 'That chap—Tintern, I think you called him—he's a funny one.'

'He's very quiet.'

'Where does he come from?'

Shirl held the mug close under the tap so that the nozzle was actually in the beer before making the final half pull for topping up. She paused, as if using all her strength on the handle, before saying: 'It's funny you should ask that, because I should think he comes from the same place as you gentlemen.'

'Oh? Where's that?'

'London. I thought you might know him.'

'There's a lot of people in London, Shirl.'

'I know that, you barmy ha'porth. But he's famous.'

Green didn't like being called barmy. He said 'How much?' in the sort of voice that denoted displeasure.

'Twelve shillings, love.'

Green didn't like the bar prices either. He felt in his pocket for a florin to add to the ten shillings he'd had ready. Masters said: 'Famous at what?'

As she put the money in the till, with her back to him, Shirl said: 'He's an architect. He does cathedrals and that sort of thing.' Immediately, Masters remembered the name. Ashbury Cathedral, consecrated two years before, furbished and decorated by famous artists and sculptors, but designed and built by Derek Tintern, the man who had made a name for himself by way of rebuilding wartorn churches and saving others from collapse. A name that had appeared often enough in the Press, but seemingly always overshadowed by some bigger name that had made a lesser contribution to gild the lily he had planted. Masters recalled reading some news item about him. Not just recently. Before Christmas. In November perhaps. What had it been about? Not architecture. Oh, yes. He remembered. A car crash. That was it. One of those motorway pile-ups. The newsmen had mentioned it. He couldn't recall all the details but he seemed to recollect it had been serious. He said: 'What's a chap like Tintern doing in Finstoft?'

Shirl laughed, throatily. 'There's no need to say it as though you thought we were heathens, love. We *have got* some churches round here, you know.'

'Sorry. He's rebuilding them?'

'One. I don't suppose he'd look at the others, but St Botolph-le-Toft's one of those ancient monuments. It's got all sorts of things people like him's interested in. In the old days it used to be right at the river's edge, but it isn't now.'

'They've moved it?' said Green.

'Don't be daft, lad. The river's moved. No. In the old days, hundreds of years ago—would it be when the Saxons were here?—it had an old stone tower where they kept a look-out for those Norsemen coming. I think he said there was a wood church there then that got burnt down. Then William the Conqueror came and they built a stone church. Or something of the sort.'

Masters said: 'Saxon tower and Norman nave. That must be a rare combination. No wonder Tintern's interested. What's he doing?'

'Don't ask me, love. Pumping cement into the walls or something. I know he said he was like a dentist trying to save a bad tooth. Drilling and filling, he called it.' She moved away as a small group of newcomers came down the stairs. Masters looked at his watch. 'We'd better have dinner now if we're going to be ready and waiting for Dr Swaine when he comes. Come on. Drink up.'

Green led the way up the stairs. 'That barmaid's getting too big for her ham bags. Something about her'll have to be taken down a bit.'

'As long as it isn't the ham bags,' Masters said. 'And talking of ham, doesn't this part of the world produce beech-fed ham? A good steak of beech-fed gammon would go down well for dinner.'

'Beech-fed?' said Brant.

Masters waited to see if Green would, or could, explain. To his great surprise, Green did so. He said: 'Haven't you ever read *Ivanhoe*, lad? Honestly, the money we waste in this country on so-called education.'

'Yes. I've read it.'

'Then you should remember how it opens. The swineherd—Garth, I think—was feeding his pigs on beech mast in the forest. And why? Because it's good pig food, that's why. And good pigs give good ham.'

'But that was in Nottingham.'

This time Green was stumped. Masters said: 'Beech trees like limestone, and there's limestone round here. You take a drink of water and you'll find it hard as Old Nick.'

Masters didn't get his ham. Instead he took the head waiter's recommendation—baked latchet. A fish he'd never heard of before. He was interested to learn that these brightly coloured, fleshy fish rarely reach any tables but those of the fishermen who catch them. So highly prized are they as food. He chose a lemon pudding to finish off with, and sat back, fuller than he'd felt for a long time. He said to Green: 'I feel more like going to bed than entertaining a boozy doctor.'

'*You* fixed the time.'

'I know. I'd like you with me. The others can do as they like.'

*

Dr Eric Swaine was short, stout, and very red faced. He wore a bristling military moustache and his dark hair was carefully brushed close to his head. His suit was impeccable, and his tiny shoes—a deep, dark tan—polished like mirrors. The spotless turn-ups of his shirt sleeves showed an inch below his jacket cuffs, which were folded back double, with rounded corners and matching braid edgings. At some time in the past he had lost an upper right incisor, and the gap showed dark against the whiteness of the rest. It also caused him to lisp slightly. And a lisp, added to his military tones, robbed them of any offensiveness there might otherwise have been. He talked a lot, but never wasted words, except when swearing, which he did unashamedly throughout every conversation.

'Strong ale,' he said in answer to Masters' invitation. 'Shirl knows.' He waited courteously until all three were served and then said: 'Here's to the health of your blood.' His glass was half empty when he lowered it. He turned to the bar and said: 'Same again, Shirl, girl. At the table in the corner, please.' He looked up at Masters. 'A bit of privacy won't come amiss. The folks round here grow ears as long as those on the donkeys they run on the sands in summer.' He led the way. Green looked at Masters and raised his eyebrows. Masters nodded. For once he and Green were agreed. Dr Eric Swaine was an interesting character.

Swaine edged round the table into the corner seat, carefully holding the glass high in one hand away from his body as if afraid of spattering himself. He said: 'Bloody nice to meet you chaps. This job needs fellers who know what they're about. Locals are all right, but they've not known whether they've been on their arses or elbows this last week. And as for old Scratch-me-backside—Bullimore—he gets goose-pimples if I mention a woman's knickers. Calls them underwear or nether garments or some such humbug. As far as I'm concerned what's what is what, and I hope it is with you, too.'

Masters grinned. The turkey-cock air, the seriousness of the little doctor amused him. He said: 'We like plain speech, Dr Swaine. But please remember that we have to write official reports, so keep the plain speech printable, otherwise we shall be in difficulties.'

'See what you mean. Ah! The drinks. Thanks, Shirl. Nine bob? Keep the change. And keep your eye open, too. When I give you the nod, make it the same again.' He turned to Masters. 'Now these women. All two point seveners . . .'

'What?' said Green.

'Average, middle class. Average number of kids in average middle-class families is two point seven. These five had thirteen between them. Three twos, a three and a four. Works out at two point six each.'

Green nodded. Masters said: 'Did you know any of the murdered women personally?'

'All of them, casually. One of them, Joanna Osborn, was a patient of mine.'

'Superintendent Bullimore says you have a theory about them.'

'Theory? Look, Mr Masters, I was asked to say whether they'd been sexually assaulted. That's not what was meant, but it's how it was put. What Bullimore wanted to know was whether these women had gone off into the dunes for a bit on the side—of their own free will—and if so, whether they'd got what they'd gone for.'

'And had they?'

'How could I tell? They were all married women, living with their husbands, and all still bedworthy—or nubile—if you prefer it and so, presumably, living normal married lives. And they'd been buried, some of them for weeks. All the indications would have perished long before they were dug up. But even if they hadn't, I wouldn't have been able to supply an answer.'

'And there were no signs of assault?'

'Not a bra strap out of place among the lot of them. They were done to death for some reason other than sex. After all, it stands to reason that a man mad enough to kill for that purpose would choose younger women.'

'All cats look grey in the dark,' commented Green.

'Maybe they do. But it would be stretching the long arm of coincidence from here to Vladivostok and back to pick haphazardly and yet get five women all of an age, all married, all the same type five times out of five.'

Masters said: 'Well, Doctor, what *is* your theory?'

'I haven't got a theory. That's your business. But I know in my bones that there's something bloody mysterious about these deaths.'

'Such as?'

'Symbolism.'

'Could you explain?'

'Well, at least *you're* prepared to listen to me.' He finished his second drink and held the empty glass high in the air. He kept it there until he'd got an answering wave from Shirl. Then he said: 'Come on, drink up. You're falling behind.'

'Count me out this round,' said Masters. 'I'll rejoin you later. But I'll not stop listening.'

'Thank God for that. Now, here's the pork and beans. The first cadaver that came to me—I forget her name . . .'

'Mrs Cynthia Baker.'

'That's the one. When I started to do the post-mortem she was pretty well covered in sand.'

'You mean you weren't called to the site where she was buried?'

'Of course I was. But I couldn't do anything there. She was so plainly dead I just took a look at her neck to make sure of the cause of death and waited to get the body on the table before going any further.'

'Sorry. I interrupted you.'

'Don't apologize. It was a pertinent point. But we'll talk about that later. However, when she arrived, I did the obvious searches. No head wounds and no sexual assault, as I told you. But I then completed dusting her off. I'd not completely cleaned her up earlier, because the sand on her exposed skin was wet and clinging, so it wouldn't come away very easily. But after I'd put a hair dryer on her, the sand dried and brushed off quite easily. I cleaned her up round the eyes and face, and then noticed something that'd escaped me before.'

'What?'

'Her nose was broken.' He took a pull at his new glass as if waiting for a reaction to his words. He got it.

Green said: 'So what?'

Swaine put the glass down and said: 'It'd been broken deliberately.'

'So she *was* swiped, after all.'

'No.'

'What, then? Oh, I know. She was gagged, and the upper edge of the gag caught across her nose and broke it.'

'That's what I thought at first, but I was wrong. There was no sign of gagging or binding, but there was a bruise on the exterior of the left nostril. I got the impression that it was a bruise caused by pressure rather than a sudden blow because there was no contusion, the skin was intact, and there'd been no epistaxis—nose bleeding to you. The septum was broken.'

'The septum being the soft central bone in the nose?' asked Masters.

'That's right. The interior of the nose is divided into two lateral halves by the nasal septum. If you feel your own proboscis, you'll notice that the lower half, below the bridge, is rubbery. You can push it from side to side without doing any damage. That's nature's way of protecting what sticks out from getting seriously hurt when it probes into things that don't concern it. So I was a bit surprised to find the septum broken. It had the appearance—to me—of a deliberately inflicted injury.'

'Did it? That's interesting.'

'How else would a woman get a bruise there—a bruise that didn't appear to come from a blow; that wasn't big enough to come from a fist or a weapon? I formed the impression that it had been caused by slow pressure—perhaps from a thumb.'

'But you can't be sure?'

'I couldn't. Not with the first. But I've had three more to examine since then, and every one has exactly the same bruise on the exterior of the left nostril, and every one has a fractured septum. That makes me sure. Again I say it can't be coincidence. It must be deliberate.'

'Ritual?' said Green.

Swaine nodded. 'And that's only the first bit of symbolism I've got for you. You asked me a minute or two ago if I'd seen those poor bitches in their graves.' He raised his empty glass to attract Shirl's attention, and said, without looking at them: 'I did. All four. It was pathetic, I tell you. Bloody pathetic. Here, come on. You're in on this round.'

'My turn,' said Masters. 'But it's my last. I've not had a subtotal gastrectomy like you. Too much alcohol takes its toll.'

Swaine grinned. 'You're as sober as I am, and that's saying something. You give me the impression of being needle sharp. Not one of the types that'll close his eyes to facts just to keep his nose clean. Thank you, Shirl. Just put it there, my dear. On the beer mat.'

As soon as Shirl had gone, Masters said: 'What was it about the graves that you noticed? More features common to all?'

Swaine said: 'If you were going to bury a body—presumably in a hurry—what sort of hole would you dig?' 'A slit trench,' Green said without hesitation.

'So would I and, I suspect, so would most other people. For one thing it's the easiest way to get down deep with the least amount of labour. But our friend obviously wasn't interested in depth—and so he obviously wasn't concerned in hiding his handiwork beyond hope of early discovery. He dug relatively shallow saucer-shaped depressions.'

'That shows he's a nut,' said Green.

'It does. But he's not a loony. He's a methodical nut. The nose business proves that, and one must suppose he had—to him—an adequate reason for doing it. And he had a reason for digging circular graves. He laid his victims out with their arms and legs stretched wide like that Da Vinci drawing of a man in a circle. Why he wanted to do that, I can't guess. But he did it.'

'More symbolism or ritual,' Masters said. 'It's interesting to hear, but I wonder how useful it's going to be in helping us to find this joker? Don't misunderstand me, Doctor. I'm not doubting the value of *your* facts and deductions. I'm simply thinking how ill-equipped men such as Green and myself are to deal with—what? A psychotic murderer, I suppose you'd call him?'

'Deal with? *You* won't have to deal with him. *You've* only got to catch him; and then some poor bastard of a psychiatrist will have to try and deal with him for the next twenty or thirty years.'

'So I've only got to catch him. Thanks.'

'Don't get me wrong. I know your job's as large a slice of tough titty as it would be most men's misfortune to meet in twice a lifetime. But if you're successful it's over and done with in a limited time. If you fail, you're withdrawn. Either way you're out of it fairly soon. But criminal psychiatry is a life sentence for the doctor as well as for the murderer.'

'It sounds as if you're interested in that particular field.'

'I am. But I'm restraining my interest. As yet, it's easier to research in psychiatry than to treat cases. What I mean is, it's easier to formulate apparently successful theories than to get successes in practice. And you know what? I've analysed myself and come to the conclusion that I'm a type that likes successes to spur me on. If I had to spend years slogging away without visible or measurable success I'd need psychiatry myself. That's not to say I won't in any case, some day, but the trick-cyclist who puts me to sleep's going to hear some ripe stories.'

Masters thought that in spite of his alleged ability to drink as much as he liked without becoming intoxicated, Swaine was becoming less staccato, more smoothly mellow, than he had been on arrival. The Chief Inspector had taken a liking for the little man; his lisp, his constant flow of invective, and the gestures he used to punctuate the conversation. He wondered whether he should ask Hill to drive the doctor home, or whether this would be taken as indicating a disbelief in his drink-assimilating powers. The matter was settled for him. Shirl called time. By now the customers in the Sundowner had shrunk to a handful. Swaine got to his feet and said: 'Knowing I was about to consort with the police tonight, I took care to come by taxi. It should be calling back for me about now.' He took a neatly tooled card case from his pocket and handed a card to Masters. 'My address. I expect we'll be meeting again, won't we? Call or phone any time. I'll be glad to hear what progress you make.'

They escorted him up the stairs. He was steady as a rock, but Masters noted that he used the balustrade and that he trod flat-footed on the treads.

After they had seen Swaine away Masters said to Green: 'Are you too heavy with beer to talk for half an hour?'

'What about?'

'Strangulation.'

Green grimaced. 'You think of the nicest things at the nicest times. What's eating you now?'

Masters said: 'Hell! It doesn't matter if your guts have gone sour on you. Get to bed and sleep it off.'

Green obviously considered this a slur on his capacity for holding his beer. He said: 'I'm as fit as you are. But you've got no evidence to discuss. I heard what the doc said. There's nothing that can't wait till morning.'

'I've told you. Go to bed.'

The tactics worked. The more Masters urged him to go, the more he was determined to stay. Green said: 'If it's noses you're worried about, don't. It happens every day to boxers, rugby players and people who walk into doors. Broken noses are as common as black eyes.'

'So they may be, although I doubt it. If you *are* going to talk, come to my room.' Green followed him along the silent, carpeted corridor. As Masters stood aside to let him enter first, Green said: 'What exactly did Swaine record as the cause of death? Old Bullimore was gassing about them being throttled. To me that means strangulation—squeezing the wind-pipe until they pass out.'

Masters offered Green the easy chair and took the upright one himself. He began to fill his pipe. 'In each case Swaine has given the cause of death as asphyxia due to manual strangulation.'

'Definitely manual? Not a cord or a nylon stocking?'

'Manual. That's why those noses worry me. I'm not too familiar with these cases. In fact I've never dealt with manual strangulation before. I expect you have?'

'Two or three times.'

'Then let's pool our knowledge—your practice and my theory. Would you like to begin?'

Green lit a Kensitas, leaned back and crossed his legs. Masters thought he was beginning to look old. Not surprising, considering the lateness of the hour, the alcohol he had drunk, and the fact that they had just finished one murder inquiry and had now been pitchforked into another without any break.

Green said: 'I can tell you this, for sure, and that is that any strangulation victim fights like the clappers.'

'Even women?'

'They're usually women. And don't run away with the idea that women are feeble, even when they're getting on a bit. I've known some of these real old biddies—the ones that keep little shops and the like—scrap like tom-cats when it comes to fighting for their lives. They find hidden reserves of strength. We all do when we've got to.'

'Fine. Now what exactly would we hope to find by way of evidence to prove they've put up a fight?'

Green pouted, thinking. 'Well, my memory's not too bad . . .'

'You know it's like a computer. What d'you remember?'

'In every case, the victim struggled like a bastard to pull or force the strangler's hands from round her neck. Why the hell nobody teaches girls from the age of five upwards to knee an attacker in the crutch or scrape down his shins with a shoe and stamp on the top of his foot, I can't understand. They're sure ways of freeing yourself.'

'We'll suggest to the education authority that it's made a compulsory part of the curriculum. Now, what marks were there in your cases?'

'Scratches round the neck—digging in with the nails to get behind the strangler's fingers.'

Masters got up, and went to the wash basin and filled his tooth glass with cold water. Sipping it he came back to his chair. 'What would you say if I told you that Swaine's reports make no mention of neck scratches?'

Green thought for a moment. 'I'd look at the lists of clothing to see if they were all wearing gloves. Come to think of it, they would be, on nights like this, out in the open.'

Masters said: 'None of them was wearing gloves when found.'

'You're sure?'

'Absolutely. So it means that the murderer removed them from the victims after death. Right?'

'Must have done. Unless he *did* put them out before he throttled them.'

Masters reached for the file and skimmed through the reports. He looked up. 'There's not a single instance of stunning and no evidence of drugging—chloroform pads and what-have-you. No burning round the mouths or traceable injection sites.'

'You say there are no scratches on the necks. What about bruises? The scratches were usually running down the neck, made by the finger-nails. In a violent struggle, gloved hands would cause bruises where the scratches should be.'

Masters rubbed the warm bowl of his pipe on the outside of one nostril. It seemed to soothe him. He said: 'No bruises either. At least not like the ones you suggest.'

'O.K. What marks were there?'

'Bruises in the larynx. Fracture of either the hyoid bone or the thyroid cartilage in every case. They are typical signs of strangulation. That much I do know.'

'This is getting to be funny—or not funny, depending on which way you look at it.'

Masters, thumbing again through the report said: 'In two cases there was haemorrhage in the epiglottis, and in one a bruise on the thyroid gland.' He went on reading the notes. 'And the other symptoms Swaine's listed back up his cause of death. They're classic signs of strangulation, aren't they? Blue or purple lips and ears; nails changed colour; froth at the mouth; tongue forced outwards?'

Green nodded. 'You've picked a right one here. The women were all strangled manually. There's no doubt about that. But there are no signs of struggling in any of the cases. This should mean that the victims were knocked out before strangulation took place. But there aren't any discernible signs of this, either. So where do we go from here? Oh—and there's that point about the gloves. Women who could afford them wouldn't go without on a cold night?'

'We must assume the murderer removed them. Otherwise, at least some of them would have had gloves on. All four without would be an unlikely coincidence; but it makes sense if we attribute it to one of the quirks of this particular character, who seems to set a pattern in everything he does.'

Green got to his feet. 'I might have known you'd have found something to make things difficult. You usually do. Now we've got to decide when is a strangler not a strangler. I'll leave *you* to sleep on it since *you* thought it up.'

In bed, Masters lay in a half sleep. Not heavy enough with drink to fall into dreamless slumber, but too tired to concentrate on the problems presented by the day, he hovered in limbo, mind active but wandering. He saw five women whirling, spreadeagled in saucers, then descending like electron microscope visuals of snowflake crystals: all perfect patterns of compass point arms and orbs. But the only face he could recognize was the fifth one. Four were middle-aged and unknown to him. The fifth was young and lovely. As she descended her face remained behind the arms of the snowflake. The shadows of the crystal across her features turned into a grille—a prison grille. It was Joan Parker. The girl he wanted, but whom he had put behind bars. For a moment he was tormented by memory, then a military voice with a lisp said: 'I've seen them all. All those poor bitches.' He recognized the voice. The tiny doctor . . . the half-pint doctor. Yes, that was it. A half doctor. And what use was a half doctor? Masters decided that a half doctor was no use unless . . . yes! He himself would have to be the other half doctor. That would make a full doctor and give all the answers. Joan Parker appeared again and smiled. An encouraging smile. She floated away behind her snowflake and whirled away in her saucer. He could hear the wind. The high wind. And feared for her safety. He tried to follow her with his eyes, but she went suddenly. The doctor lisped: 'We'll work together. Psychotic criminals . . . methodical loonies . . . poor bitches.'

Masters didn't hear the church clock strike the next hour.

Chapter Three

The next morning the wind had died down and the rain had gone. Masters stood at his bedroom window at half past seven and looked out across the roadway, the gardens and the promenade. The tide was out, and that was as much as he could tell, because darkness still lingered, acting as rearguard to the spell of grey weather, reluctant to let the light come back to a wretched world. But he sensed that he would be able to operate in the open without too much discomfort. The thought cheered him. He turned to the basin and started to lather his face. He shaved automatically, concentrating on the day's work, so that by the time he was dressed he couldn't remember using or cleaning his razor. But a glance in the mirror reassured him. When his morning tea arrived—ordered for eight o'clock—he was folding the new suit he had worn for the past few days, to be sent for valeting.

Green was his usual cheerless self at breakfast. He said: 'Most pubs serve boneless kippers these days. I'd've had boiled eggs if I'd known they weren't filleted.'

'They don't smoke 'em these days, you know. They use smoke flavouring,' Brant said.

'Garn tittle. How'd they get this colour on a two-eyed steak if it wasn't smoked?'

'Artificial colouring matter. I know a chap who works in that line. They even export smoke flavour to Norway and Denmark.'

Green pushed his plate away. He'd made a messy job of his fish. He went on to toast and marmalade. Masters said to Hill: 'Don't forget P.C. Garner. He should be arriving fairly soon.'

Green said: 'Where'll he sit in the car?'

'In the back. I thought you and I would walk along the front. The others can take the car round by the road and meet us where the track joins the embankment.'

'It's all of two miles. We'll be wasting time.'

'We'll also be getting to know the area. I want to see where we are. This place is new to me. And the ozone'll do us good.'

Masters and Green set out before Garner arrived. For half a mile they walked along made-up road, which came to an end in a turning circle for the buses. After that there was the embankment. A wall, faced on the seaward side with grey limestone rock roughly set in cement, and sloping down at about forty-five degrees to the shore. Here the sand was covered in a ridge of weed with all manner of flotsam sticking up from it. At one spot several whole grapefruit—perhaps jettisoned by some idle ship's cook—stood out round and yellow. Baulks of timber of all sizes, laced with black-green bladder wrack; small pieces of wood, their ends rounded by the abrasive action of sand and water, and the soft wood worn out from between the heavy grain, lay thrown up by the waves. Rounded knobs of coal; areas of coal slack, washed bright and free of dust. Shells, mostly white, with the dark blue of mussels here and there. Broken bottles, boxes, paper, rag. It was a rubbish dump, but Masters thought it interesting. The harvest of the sea. The contents of gash chutes washed ashore, cleansed by contact with angry water and no longer malodorous. Between this line of debris and the water's edge was an expanse of wet sand nearly half a mile wide. Sand ridged by the waves into a perfectly symmetrical pattern, with hollows deep enough to hold small elongated pools that glittered like beaten pewter under a floodlight. Green said: 'What's happened to the water? They've pulled the plug out.'

Masters said, absently: 'Spring tides. Very high at full tide, very low at ebbs. We're now between times.'

'How do you know?'

'At four o'clock yesterday afternoon the tide was full. You get two tides a day on the east coast, at about twelve and a half hour intervals. That means there was another tide this morning that would be full about four thirty. This afternoon it will be full at five. If we're here many days we'll find the water up at this time in the morning.'

Green grunted and said nothing. He walked along whistling at gulls that were wheeling low overhead and making sudden glides down to snatch at debris in the seaweed. Masters was thinking of patterns. Of his conversation with Swaine. Of a half-remembered dream. Of this sand figured like intricately cut glass. All patterns. And he could make nothing of them as yet.

The top of the embankment was tarmac. Thin enough to show the underlying sand where a pot hole had broken the surface. On the landward side was winter plough. Sandy, but with a pattern still clearly visible and not obliterated by rain and wind. He guessed the two had militated against each other. The rain had bound the soil too strongly for the wind to dislodge. Drainage ditches, without hedges, but with a narrow band of coarse green growth on each bank, cut across the area and drained through a sluice in the embankment to the foreshore. A discoloured torrent that cut a course for itself for twenty yards in the sand and then petered out, spreading in a shallow pool over the ridges.

They walked in silence for some minutes. The wind was still fresh enough to reveal itself in patterns where there was any grass exposed to it. It could still make the cheeks tingle. The grey day started to brighten in a watery sort of way. Two or three miles out a couple of trawlers were fighting their way into the estuary. The cry of the gulls was raucous but unobtrusive in this great open space.

Green said: 'There's the car.' He pointed. A track, as yet invisible, and delineated only by the movement of the car, curved round from half a mile inland to meet the embankment. Masters saw a small square notice-board on a pole a quarter of a mile ahead and guessed it indicated the end of the sea wall and the junction with the track. He was right. Inside five minutes they had joined the three in the car. Before them stretched a line of dunes four or five feet high and behind these, the bungalow village, built haphazardly, with no semblance of order. The huts were painted many colours, faced in all directions, were of different sizes and of varying pretentiousness. Each had a wired-in garden area—sand, with the uprights for children's swings and clothes-line poles standing dotted about.

Green said: 'I see they've all got an Elsan Hall.' At the end of each garden was a tiny hut. Brant said: 'D'you know, I thought they were tool sheds,' and laughed at himself.

Masters said to Garner: 'Do you happen to know where the graves are?'

Garner was in civilian clothes. He was wearing a belted mackintosh and gumboots. His head was bare, and the remains of his skimpy grey hair were blowing in the wind, straggling over his bald patch and his ears. He had high colouring, underlined by a pallor still remaining from his recent illness. But his eyes were bright and smiling. He said: 'They've all got hessian screens round, sir. But the wind could have blown them over.'

'Was there no guard out here?'

'Yes, sir. In a Panda car stationed just where we are now until eight o'clock. Superintendent Bullimore asked me to tell you he couldn't spare the car any more. But the exact places where the bodies were lying are marked by two sticks. White at the head and black at the foot.'

'Right,' Masters said. 'Are we ready? There should be one grave between the dunes and the water line. That should be easy to find, so we'll start there.'

The hessian was wet and soggy. The four corner poles of the screen had all bent inwards under the weight and the force of the wind. The grave was still there, and in spite of it being sand, there was water in the bottom. Masters gingerly moved the screen and went inside. He said to Green: 'What d'you think? Three feet deep?'

'Hardly. What's been dug out has been piled round the sides. It's got flattened a bit, but I wouldn't put it at much more than two feet.'

'And six feet across?'

'About that.'

'How long would it take to dig?'

'It's amazing how fast you can go in this sort of stuff when you're in a hurry. I suppose he had a shovel? Yes, he must have had. In my day I reckon I could have done it in less than twenty minutes.'

'You should know. Alamein and all that.' He opened the big scale map. 'Now, here's the cross marking this one. How do we know it's right? Measure from the nearest bungalow, I suppose.'

Surprisingly, Green took over. He said: 'We'll have to do a resection. I'll have the compass first.'

Hill handed over the heavy prismatic. Green said: 'The trouble with these big plans is they don't cover enough space to get really decent rays.'

'This is all Greek to me.'

Green said: 'Never mind. You'll learn. Now, is that sewage outfall tower marked? Right. All metal out of the way?' He put the compass to his eye and took the bearing of the conical lattice tower standing out of the water a mile away. He murmured: 'Two nine seven. Take away a hundred and eighty. Gives us a hundred and seventeen. Make a note of that, somebody.'

Brant scribbled the figure down. Green said: 'Now I want something as near at right angles as possible to get a good, clean cut.' He pointed back along the track the car had used. He said: 'What's that low, brick building yonder?'

Garner said: 'The Golf Club, sir.'

'Is it on the map?'

Masters said: 'It's here.' He was trying to follow Green's manœuvres. Up to now he hadn't succeeded. Green took another shot with the compass. 'Two four eight,' he said. 'Take off a hundred and eighty. Gives us sixty-eight. Got that?'

Brant nodded.

Green took the map from Masters and the protractor from Hill. He said: 'I need a table. We'll have to go back to the car and use the bonnet.'

While the others held down the map corners, Green drew lines at the back bearings he had given Brant from the sewage tower and the Golf Club House. They crossed almost at right angles an eighth of an inch away from Bullimore's original cross. He turned to Masters. 'Six inches to a mile. That means an inch is roughly three hundred yards. An eighth of an inch would be what? Between thirty-five and forty yards? That's about how far out the first grave is.'

'You're sure?'

'No. But I can test by taking a third ray and getting a triangle of error if you like.' Green was enjoying himself. Masters wondered where he had learned this particular skill. Green gave him the answer without being asked. He said: 'Of course, when we did survey in the Gunners we used directors, and they're more accurate than compasses. But I put the magnetic deflection on, so I shouldn't be more than half a degree out in my bearings.'

He returned to the grave and took a shot at a church tower, nearly four miles away, and just inside the bounds of the map. He had some difficulty in seeing, with one eye closed, and the other squinting through the hair-line slit. The tower was the same grey as the sky behind it, and it was some minutes—after resting his arm twice—before he was satisfied where the three lines on the map crossed. Green said: 'Make a dot in the middle of that, and you'll be bang on.'

Masters said: 'So Bullimore *was* about thirty yards out. Not bad for by guess and by God.'

Green said, amiably enough for him: 'Not bad at all. But I bet he wasn't so hot on the others. This was easy. Right on the shore line. He could only make a mistake east and west. The north-south line was fixed for him.'

'Can we plot the others?'

'We can. But why the hell should we? What's the use of knowing to within a yard where they were dumped?'

'Can you tell me why the murderer lugged his victims' bodies in all directions before burying them? Say he came by car. He would be obliged to park where our wagon is now. Yet the graves he dug are dotted about. Why not put them all together? As close to the car as possible? And save transporting dead weight over soft sand—which is difficult to walk on at the best of times.'

Green replied: 'How d'you know they were dead when they arrived? He could have walked them off into the dunes and killed them where they stopped. They just didn't happen to go in the same direction each time.'

Masters could see the force of this argument, and agreed that Green had every possibility of being right. 'But,' he said, 'remember Swaine's theory last night. Symbolism. I can't ignore the fact that the same thread runs right through every one of the murderer's actions. I've looked at this plan, with Bullimore's crosses on it, and I can see no rhyme nor reason in the dispersal of the bodies. And nobody has found the fifth victim. For all we know she could be miles from here. May well be, if your theory is right. And yet, if that were so, it would be the first inconsistency, wouldn't it? So, on the off chance that it *will* help us, let's plot the others carefully.'

'O.K. You're the boss. Come on, lads. We'll need the fifty foot this time.' Hill held it out. A long tape in a brown leather cover, big as a tea plate, and an inch deep.

'Can I leave it to you?' said Masters.

Green nodded, and said to Garner: 'We're going clockwise round to finish up here again. I want you to go to the next grave. Here, see. Southeast. About two hundred yards away. When you get there, stand right beside it and hold up a white handkerchief. If I can see it, we'll be O.K. If not, you'll have to tie it on the end of one of the sticks round the grave and hold it up. Right? Off you go then.'

Green turned to Masters. 'This may take a long time. If they're not intervisible, we'll have to do dog legs round obstacles.'

'What does that mean?'

'Plot intermediate points by bearing and distance. And I don't like that much. Apart from the time it'll take I'm liable to get up to half a degree error in every bearing as I told you.'

'Can you judge how inaccurate it will be when you've finished?'

Green lit a Kensitas. 'I can tell you now. It'll be bloody inaccurate. But I'm going to close on this first grave at the end, so we'll be able to see exactly. Then, to iron out the error, I could go round again, anti-clockwise, and see what comes up.'

Masters said: 'Do your best. If I can be of help I'll be nosing round. Give me a shout.' He waited a few minutes to fill his pipe and to watch Green dispose his forces. After a bit of to-ing and fro-ing by Brant, carrying messages to Garner to get the handkerchief higher, Green was able to take a direct bearing to the second grave. Then followed the business of measuring by Brant and Hill. Green was taking great care to see that their fifty feet of tape were always in the direct line between himself and the handkerchief. He controlled them by a series of arm signals. Right arm outstretched—move to the right. Arm slapped down, stop. Left arm up—move gently to the left. Stop. Mark the spot. Measure the next fifty feet. Masters could see that the exercise would take some time. With his pipe burning well in the wind, he turned to the bungalows and trudged over the sand towards them.

They were depressing. Wooden huts with corrugated iron roofs. Eyeless because the windows were boarded up. Tatty because the paint, mainly green and white, was flaking and faded, sapped of its nature by the salt-laden air and sun. Wooden huts on stilts to keep them clear of the sand. Masters looked more closely at these foundations. Some were of squared timber, but most were large, round, wooden blocks, eighteen inches in diameter and a foot deep. Small flights of two or three wooden steps up to front doors—each with a name reminiscent of fictional suburbia: Crow's Nest, Dun Roamin, Sandy Nook—on to verandas, where sand had drifted against palings in narrow slopes like wedges of cheese. He walked round the back of the nearest one. Here a gutter had been added to the roof and a downspout leading into a forty-gallon oil drum with a distorted wooden lid. The recent rain had caused it to overflow, and the sand around it was darker and wetter than the rest. There were padlocks on the shutters and the door. He guessed there would be four rooms. One with a fireplace, because a tin chimney with a coolie-hat on top stood up a foot above the roof.

He looked around. On some bungalows there were television aerials; and one or two had car ports, some tailor made, others constructed of sections of old air raid shelter. But nowhere could he see any article which suggested that for several months in the year hundreds of families lived here and enjoyed themselves. The owners had taken great care to see that the scavengers didn't get rich at their expense.

As he moved about, he came across Garner, erecting a banderole for his handkerchief at the third grave. Masters said: 'I've never seen those round wooden things before. What are they?'

Garner said: 'Fishing bobbins, sir. They've got a hole down the middle like a cotton bobbin. They're threaded on to a metal foot rope and roll along the sea bed as the trawlers fish. At least they did. They use metal ones now. But those old wooden ones are useful for all sorts of things. I've got one at home I use for a chopping block when I'm cutting kindling.'

Masters thanked him. He looked into the grave. White and black sticks about five feet apart. He walked on to the fourth grave. The same sticks. He stood for a moment. Lit his pipe. Then lined himself up behind the white stick, looking directly over the black one. He could see the distant outskirts of Finstoft. He noted the building in line with his view. He returned to the first grave and repeated the manœuvre. The line of the white and black sticks again picked up the same building. Interested, he trudged round the remaining two graves. The same result. Green by now was on his last lap. As he stood signalling to the sergeants, Masters told him of this new discovery.

Green said: 'All lined up, are they?'

'No. They concentrate on the one building.'

Green slapped his hand to his thigh and made a pushing signal with both hands to tell the sergeants to move on. Then he said: 'They only appear to concentrate. That building's so far away that the slightest divergence out of parallel would make the lines miss it. They're lined up, I reckon.'

'Could you use your compass to tell me in exactly what direction?'

'Nothing easier.'

Green finished his traverse and again using the bonnet of the car as his table, plotted the various bearings and distances. His work was good. By the time he'd finished he had an irregular rectangle with a grave at each corner, except the first. Here he had a slight gap in the lines and two crosses. He said: 'We're as near as dammit right. Not more'n fifteen yards out at any rate. Good enough?'

'Excellent, thank you.' He looked at the map. It told him nothing. There were Bullimore's marks and Green's marks and the resection rays and the traverse box. It was a hotchpotch. Reluctantly he folded it away and said: 'Now, the alignment of the graves.'

He plodded round with Green, who took shots over the head and foot sticks as marker posts. Green made notes on his Kensitas packet after each one. As they walked back to the car at the end, he said: 'Well, as near as I can tell you, the bodies were laid due east and west, with the heads pointing east. Was that what you were expecting?'

'Something of the sort. It doesn't tell us much, but it definitely corroborates Swaine's belief that symbolism is involved; and that the one we're after is a most methodical loony.'

They all got into the car for the journey back to the Estuary. Garner, sitting forward between Masters and Green on the back seat was uncomfortable, not only because of his restricted *sitzplatz*, but because of his proximity to two men who, as leaders of this particular team, had a countrywide reputation for success in difficult cases. He wondered about them. In spite of the reputation they appeared very ordinary men to him. But different in their attitudes. More professional. No local C.I.D. men had gone out and surveyed the area. And from what he had gathered from the conversation nobody had tumbled to this theory of—what was it?—symbolism? He wondered exactly what was meant by it. Perhaps if he kept his eyes and ears open he'd get to know. Meanwhile he felt more than pleased to be working with leading lights from Scotland Yard, even if it was only as dogsbody. His thoughts were interrupted by Masters who said: 'Would you like a drink, Constable, before your lunch?'

'Thanks very much, sir.'

'O.K. A quick one and then Sergeant Brant will run you home. It's twelve now. Can you get back to the Estuary by two?'

'Easily, sir.'

'Right. Here we are.'

*

The Sundowner was fairly full. They stood together—a ring of five big men—away from the bar. Green said: 'Visiting relatives this afternoon?'

Masters said: 'That's right. We'll split into pairs. I want you, Garner, to act as guide and chauffeur. And please get a list of the telephone numbers of the houses so we can make contact that way if needs be, otherwise, with only one car, some of us could be stranded for a long time.'

'Very good, sir.' Garner put his beer mug on a small table. 'Well, thanks. I'll be off now if it's all right with the sergeant.'

Brant followed him up the stairs.

Masters said: 'We've read the local reports, but I want us all to forget them. They're superficial.'

'They struck me like the minutes of a meeting of the old boy network,' said Green. 'They're all old pals round here, so they can't be objective. When you know a chap socially you can't question him close enough to bash the acne out of him, can you?'

'Substitute "exact the truth" for what you've just said and I'll agree.'

'We're slipping, aren't we, chief?' Hill said. 'Been here nearly twenty-four hours and not one suspect.'

'You remember the case we finished two days ago? We ignored the weapon there, because we'd no lead on it. But we managed to arrive by taking a roundabout route. I may be wrong, but here I feel the murderer himself is not as important as his motive. That's what I want to get at.'

'I know his motive. He's crackers. Really, seriously mad,' said Green.

'Maybe. And mental illness alone may drive a man to murder. But what causes his mental illness? That's my point. I think some powerful emotion motivated a sick man to the point where he could bear to commit five murders. Ritualistically and cunningly. And we've got to dig out the reason for that emotion, otherwise we've had it. We're not going to solve this one with fingerprints and breaking an alibi. It's going to mean some hard slogging and, unless I'm mistaken, some hefty digging into the past.'

Hill said: 'And I bet I know who's got to do most of the digging. Have we time for one more, before Sarn't Brant gets back?' Masters declined. 'We'll go for lunch. He'll be with us before we're served.'

When they were having their coffee, Masters said: 'It's no use setting out with any preconceived ideas of what you're going to hear. Obviously we want everything we can get that relates to the time each woman disappeared, but I particularly want to know whether we can establish any form of relationship between them or any common factor which links them. It doesn't matter what it is. But most of all I want to find a common, human contact, because I can see no material reason for these murders, whereas human—probably mental—conflict could account for them. Find out. If we can establish a common denominator our job's going to be a lot easier than it would be if these five women were all picked at random. But you don't need me to tell you that. Patterns in crimes help solve them. And in this particular crime there are so many patterns that I'm positive there must be a design in the selection of victims. Let's find out what it is. We may not get it today, or for a number of days. But gather the pieces, just the same.'

'What about the husbands? Are we concentrating on them to begin with?' said Brant.

'You're concentrating on everybody and everything. But chiefly consider that here are five women all of whom have lived in this area for the past forty years. I want a common factor—human if possible. Our job is to find that common factor, and to do it we have to know when it was in existence. So, as I said last night, we have to dig deep. Five women and forty years to play with. It's a big job.'

Green said: 'We'll not get round five of them today at that rate.'

'Never mind. Just do one today. As long as you get a notebook full of facts and names that can be checked with other reports to see if the lines cross. Take it steady. We'll start with the two Finstoft women—Frances Burton and Joanna Osborn—the alpha and omega in the disappearing act and numbers three and two to reappear, respectively. Hill and I'll take Burton. You and Brant tackle Osborn. They both had two children. Anything else you'd like to know?'

'Disappearance dates.'

'Oh, yes. Burton disappeared on the tenth, reported on the twelfth. Osborn disappeared on the twenty-eighth. And I'll stress this again—get a list of all their friends, past and present. At least one human contact must be there, and we want to know who it is.'

*

Saturday afternoon always had a special feeling about it for Masters. Subconsciously he believed there were certain things you could do on certain days at certain times, and certain things you could not do on certain days at certain times. He believed that after lunch on Saturdays the time for investigation and questioning stopped until Monday morning. As they drove through the streets, the sun now a little stronger and the wind a little weaker, he looked out at the women and men walking together, the family parties hurrying to bus stops, and the holiday air given by people who had shed working clothes in favour of their week-end best. It didn't seem right to him to be going to work at this time. He'd have preferred to be off duty. He was dour, because of it. The others sensed this, and there was no conversation in the car.

Garner directed them first to Rowan Tree Avenue. Away from the front of the town, tucked away to escape the worst of the north-easterly winds, the road held a mixture of detached and semi-detached houses of the better class, mostly pre-war. Each had its low fence, double gate and garage. All were well painted, with gardens which, though not yet cleared up after the winter, still bore signs of that house-proud care that tends to rob all such plots of any aspect of individuality while still leaving them as oases of colour in the midst of drabness. Even the cars, drawn up in front of each house had a sameness that depressed Masters. He would have preferred to see a few old crocks and students' bangers littered about, just to break the monotony. He had visions of Sunday mornings when, he supposed, all the men would come out with identical plastic buckets containing identical car cleanser to wash and clean these identical cars with identical sponges. He thought the men might even wear identical trousers and sweaters. He was certain they would make identical remarks to each other about the weather.

Green and Brant got down at the Osborns' house. Masters said: 'Whoever finishes first rings the other. I'll keep the car with me.'

Green nodded. Even he, the prophet of egalitarianism, seemed depressed by the equivalence of Rowan Tree Avenue, and the prospect of working on a Saturday afternoon when, as often as possible, he was accustomed to watching either Chelsea or Fulham—whichever was playing at home.

Garner pulled away, leaving Green standing on the pavement. As they turned the corner Masters looked back and saw him unfastening the gate. He wondered how Osborn and Green would get on together.

The Lincoln Road was the main highway leading south out of Finstoft. Here the houses were very much the same as in Rowan Tree Avenue, but the buses and cars speeding along gave it life, and behind the houses on the Burtons' side was a low hill with trees. Behind those on the other side, lower standing, was a playing field with glimpses of soccer strips to be seen between the buildings. Masters supposed that the Burtons must be just that little bit worse off financially than the Osborns, otherwise they might not have chosen to live on this strip of ribbon development so close to a noisy playground where the peace could be disturbed by referees' shrill whistles and spectators' shouts.

Masters and Hill went up the flagged path to the front door. Their ring was answered by a girl whom Masters thought looked about twenty; but knowing how deceptive appearances can be, he mentally catalogued her as eighteen. She was attractive. She wore slim navy-blue jeans and a paler blue, tight sweater which made her appear provocatively elegant. Her girlish—not yet quite mature—bosom stood out proud, voluptuous in its sheer precociousness. Her hair was fair, the sort that darkens gradually with time, and waved into curls too tight for Masters' taste. He preferred

Deadly Pattern

hair to bounce from exuberance in young girls. But the effect was not wasted on Hill. Masters would have wagered that in seconds after she had opened the door Hill would have been able to give a long description of her—full of unnecessary details.

Masters introduced himself.

'You'll want to see Dad?'

'If Mr Burton is in. And you too, please, Miss . . .'

'I'm Beryl. We're all at home. Dad, Robert and me. Robert's my brother.'

Masters and Hill followed her through, past the foot of the stairs, to the dining-room. The square table had been pushed back against the wall opposite the fire. This left room for two armchairs. Sitting in one was a man of about forty-five. Where the room was brown all over—brown carpet, brown curtains to the french window, brown upholstery on the easy chairs and the dining chairs—Ralph Burton was grey all over. His hair, and there was still plenty of it, had reached the stage where it was ready to whiten. His face had an ashen look: a proud face, deeply lined to give the appearance of heavy jowls even though there was little spare flesh. Grey eyes with brows not quite as dark as they'd once been. A long, spare body in a grey sweater and grey slacks with a pair of putty-coloured desert boots. He stood up as Masters entered. In the opposite chair was sprawled a sixteen-year-old lad who, at a word from his father got to his feet and switched off the television set.

Beryl said: 'Dad. This is . . . did you say Detective Chief Inspector? . . . Masters, from Scotland Yard, and Sergeant Hill.'

Burton offered his hand courteously. Masters hated hand-shakes. This time he didn't mind so much as he felt the recognition signal of a finger curl in his palm.

Burton said: 'So they've brought in the biggest of the big guns, have they?' The voice was low pitched and pleasantly modulated. Despite the grief etched on the face there was the light of humour in the eyes.

Masters said: 'The medium-sized ones, at any rate, sir.'

'You're not unknown, even to us up here in Finstoft. In fact, this morning's paper carries an account of your successful investigation in Rooksby.'

'They have to print something, don't they?' Masters said deprecatingly.

Burton said: 'And now you've come here. I must say I don't envy you your job. I've thought and thought about what's gone on here these past few weeks and I can't for the life of me see any solution—feasible or fantastic.'

'Well, perhaps a fresh mind might help. And that's why I'm here. I find gathering the threads of a case so much easier if I start afresh from the beginning and don't have to rely too much on previous reports. So if I could discuss the whole matter with you?'

'Of course. Beryl, slip into the sitting-room and switch on the heater, please.' He turned to Masters. 'We'll be much better in there.'

'I'd prefer to stay here if you don't mind, sir. Your son and daughter may be able to help us if you don't mind them sitting in.'

'Of course not. Robert's only sixteen, of course . . .'

'There'll be no grisly details, Mr Burton. Basically I'm not interested in your wife's disappearance and death at the moment, but in her life.'

'I think I understand. Where will you sit?'

'I'd like your son to sit at the table with Sergeant Hill. I'll take his chair, you take yours, and I suggest Miss Burton sits on that pouffe. Beside you. That's right.' Masters sat in the chair and stretched his legs. He said, trying to put them at their ease: 'D'you mind a pipe?'

With their permission he started to rub a fill of Warlock Flake. As he did it he said: 'Now just to get the record of recent events straight, I *will* run over the events of the tenth of January. You, Mr Burton, went to a Masonic Lodge meeting that evening, I believe?'

'That's right.'

'What time did you leave here?'

'About four o'clock. It was an installation, you see.'

'I think I can guess what that means, although I know very little about your corporate activities. How did you go? By car?'

'Taxi. We don't drink to excess, but we do have a few, so I shared a taxi both ways with Colin Mace—he lives five doors along from here.'

'He's a member of the same Lodge?'

'Yes.'

'And besides your mutual interest in Masonic affairs are your two families friendly?'

'Very. At least Frances and Mrs Mace were. But the Maces have no children, so our two weren't involved in the friendship.'

'Long standing?'

'Connie Mace and Frances were at school together, and have been fairly close ever since.'

'Was it coincidence they found themselves living so close to each other after marriage?'

'I don't understand the question.'

'They were friends at school and—as you put it—fairly close thereafter. As close friends did they arrange to live near each other, or was it coincidence that their two husbands bought almost adjoining properties.'

'Oh, I see. No. I've given you the wrong impression. For a few years, after leaving school, they didn't see much of each other. Then Frances and I married and moved in here. About a year later Colin and Connie bought their house, and the girls reassumed their old friendship. But it was quite by chance that their house fell empty when it did.'

'Thank you. Please don't think I'm being pedantic, but accuracy here will help. I'm sure of that.'

'I thought we were speaking generally. Sorry.'

'Generally, perhaps, but not loosely. But to get on. Did anything extraordinary happen at the installation?'

'Nothing.'

'Did you leave the Lodge for any purpose during the evening?'

'No.'

'What's the name and address of your Tyler?'

Beryl giggled. She said: 'You do ask funny questions. Dad gets his suits at . . .'

Burton said: 'Quiet, Beryl.' He looked over to Masters. 'I thought you didn't know much about our activities.'

'I don't. But I happen to know what a door-keeper's called, even if your daughter thinks I've got a cockney accent.'

She blushed. 'Oh, I *am* sorry. I thought you meant . . .'

Her father said: 'Never mind, Beryl.' He turned to Masters again. 'His name's Wilson. There's a small hotel attached to the Temple. He runs the hotel—the Freemason's Arms in Cobbald Street.'

'Thank you. Now what time did you get back here that night?' Burton paused before replying. Masters had demonstrated that he expected accuracy and was prepared to get an independent check on all answers. Burton was taking care. He said: 'I can't say to the minute. But we broke up at eleven, and as we'd ordered the taxi for then, Colin and I hurried out. Say five past. And it takes about seven minutes to get here. We both got out at Colin's, and I walked the little bit to our gate. So I'd say I actually got in at a quarter past eleven.'

'Good. Which taxi firm did you use?'

Hill made a note of the hire firm. Masters said: 'You came in, expecting to find your wife here?'

'Yes. She'd not said she was going out.'

'Was the house in good order?'

'Just as I would expect to find it. A light in the hall. One in here. The fire going and some of the children's belongings strewn about.'

'But no Mrs Burton?'

'No sign of Frances at all.'

'What did you do?'

'I called her. Then when she didn't answer I went upstairs to see if she'd gone to bed or was having a bath.'

'Then what?'

'I thought she'd slipped along to keep Connie company during the evening, expecting me to call in there when we came back.'

'So?'

'I hadn't called in, so I thought she'd probably be gassing to Colin, and be ready to come if I fetched her. So I went along there. Connie hadn't seen her that day.'

'I see. Now what about Beryl and Robert? Where were they?'

'It was the party season. They were here when I left at four o'clock, but I knew they would be going out later and not coming in until possibly one o'clock.'

Masters said to Beryl. 'Were you out with your brother?'

'I wasn't out *with* him. We were at the same party.'

Robert said: 'She was with that long-haired Hampden chap. A fine boy friend he turned out to be. Wouldn't even see her home. I had to do it. *And* I had to wait while he kissed her before we could start back.'

'So you arrived together. At what time?'

'Nearly half past one. We walked.'

'Thank you. Now back to you, Mr Burton. You found an empty house, and your wife wasn't with Mrs Mace. What did you do?'

'I came back here, half expecting to find her here by then. I thought she must have gone to see some other friends and had lost count of the time.'

'But she wasn't here.'

'No. I looked round in case she'd left a note. She hadn't, so I rang her mother to see if she'd gone there for the evening. No luck.'

'Did you ring anywhere else?'

'No.'

'Why not?'

'It was getting late. I didn't want to wake all our friends in the district.' Privately Masters thought that Burton's real reason was the fact that he didn't want to give his friends the idea his wife had walked out on him.

Masters relit his pipe. 'What next, Mr Burton?'

'I'm afraid I went to bed.' It was a reply that even had Masters surprised for a minute. He said: 'Just like that?'

'Well, as I told you, I'd had a few drinks and I was tired. I'd no idea where Frances had gone, so I didn't see what I could do.'

'Did it occur to you to ring the police?'

'Have you any idea what trouble it would have caused if I had rung the police, and Frances had arrived home ten minutes later?'

Masters said that as he'd never had the pleasure of knowing Mrs Burton, he was unable to imagine what her reactions would have been. But Burton's reply had confirmed Bullimore's description of the area and its people. Apparently Frances Burton would have given her husband no credit for considering her safety above everything else. She would only have been concerned about the loss of face occasioned by referring her absence to the police. He said: 'You went to bed and slept?'

'Soundly. The drink saw to that.'

'You didn't hear your children come in?'

'No. They're always very quiet when they're late. I wouldn't expect to.'

'So what happened then?'

'The next morning the children were as surprised as I was at their mother's disappearance. They assured me she had been her usual self when they left her the evening before.'

Masters turned to Beryl: 'Is that so?'

'Yes. She ironed my evening stole for me just before we went, and said she was going to make coffee and watch television after we'd gone.'

'At what time did you leave?'

'Ten to eight.'

'Who washed up next morning?'

'I did,' said Robert. 'Beryl had to go to work. I was on holiday.'

'Still at school?'

He nodded.

Masters said: 'Can you remember? Did your mother make coffee and leave a dirty cup and saucer or coffee-pot?'

'No. She didn't. But that doesn't mean she didn't have coffee. Mum always rinsed and dried her cups herself when she had a drink at odd times.'

'I see. Thank you.' He turned to Burton: 'What about her clothes? Did you check those?'

'I did,' said Beryl. 'She'd taken her heavy coat, head scarf and gloves, and she was wearing black court shoes.'

'What happened that next day? What steps did you take to trace your wife?'

'I stayed at home from the office in the morning and rang everybody I could think of, and I went through Frances' address book.'

'She'd left it behind? Where was her handbag?'

'That's just it,' said Beryl. 'She didn't take one. Just her purse—slipped in her pocket, I expect.'

'Was that a habit of hers?'

'When she was only going out for a short while, and didn't expect to need her bag.'

'Well, what we can assume so far is that Mrs Burton went willingly to wherever she was going, that she expected to be back quite quickly, and she didn't expect to be going far. Now, Beryl, you're a woman. What set of circumstances would drag you out like that on a January night, presumably without warning?'

Beryl considered this for a moment and then said: 'A boy friend with a car, calling to take me for . . .' She glanced sideways at her father. '. . . for a drink. What I mean is, Mum knew nobody would be back very early, and if somebody she knew phoned her or called, she probably thought she could slip out for an hour or so.'

'Do you mean without anybody knowing?' asked Masters.

'Well . . . no. I meant without her having to explain to Dad or to us.'

Burton said with a smile: 'Are you suggesting, young lady, that your mother had clandestine boy friends?'

'She may have had. But that's not what I'm trying to say. In a family you've always got to explain everything you do. Say where you're going and who with.'

'I should think so,' said Burton.

'But, Dad, don't you know how ghastly it is to have to do it all the time?'

Masters understood. He was a bachelor, accountable to no one for his actions. He could imagine Mrs Burton, happy enough, perhaps, with her family, but just longing to do something, go out, on her own sometime, without explanations to husband and children. It seemed to him that Beryl may have—in her immature way—put her finger on a reason for her mother's going out that evening. He said: 'Cast your mind back. What happened exactly that evening? Robert, you were here, on holiday. Beryl, you came in from work, for your tea. Right?'

Beryl nodded. Robert said: 'We just had crumpets and spready cheese with toasted scones and Christmas cake. Mum said she wouldn't cook as Dad wouldn't be home for a hot meal and we'd be having supper out.'

'Good. Then what?'

Beryl said: 'I had a bath.'

'You didn't help to wash up?'

She looked across at Robert who shook his head.

'No.'

'Do you usually help?'

'Always.'

'Even on party nights?'

'Yes.'

'Why not this night?'

'I don't know. Mum told me to get my bath so that Bobby could get his in good time.'

Masters turned to Robert. 'What did you do at washing-up time?'

'Mum told me to clean my shoes and put the ironing-board up for her to press Beryl's stole.'

'Good. That's clear. Now obviously your mother didn't let you off the washing up because you were going to a party. That wasn't her usual habit, and there could be no reason for her doing so on this particular night unless she either felt that as you'd only had nursery tea there was not much washing up to do or—and this is pure speculation—she wanted you to be away well on time for reasons of her own.'

'I offered to dry for her but she chased me off,' said Robert. 'All she kept saying was: "Now come along, Bobby, you mustn't keep Beryl waiting." I remember telling her that that Hampden bloke was calling for Beryl, but she said: "Never mind that, just do as I say and hurry up!"'

Masters looked across at Burton. 'As I said a moment ago, sir, this comes within the realm of speculation, but from your children's accounts I would guess that Mrs Burton had a pre-arranged engagement for that evening.

About eight o'clock, I should say, judging from her anxiety to hustle them.'

'If she had, I knew nothing of it.'

'Nor who could have given her an invitation?'

'No.'

'Then I must try to find out. Would you—all three of you—please make me a list of everybody your wife knew in the district?'

'Just in the district?'

'I think so. At any rate for the moment. But may I suggest that while Beryl and Robert are dealing with up-to-date contacts which they will know well enough, you cast your mind back. Go back as far as the time you first met your wife and write down those of her friends you can remember her mentioning, and your own friends—male and female—at that time.'

'That's a tall order—twenty years and more.'

'Not as tall as you might think. Most families have a snapshot album. Have you?'

Beryl said: 'There's a dress-box full of photos on top of the spare-room wardrobe.'

'Excellent. They'll help your father recall the old days and old faces. Beryl, will you and Robert fetch the photos, paper and pencils, please.'

As soon as the children were out of the room, Masters said to Burton: 'Now, sir. Your relationship with your wife. Was it good?'

'As far as I could tell, it was excellent. I mean, we cohabited normally, we did most things together, we got along and agreed on most things. As for other men in Frances' life—well, I don't think there were any, otherwise I'd be suspecting somebody of her murder.'

'Would you?'

'What do you mean?'

'You didn't report your wife's disappearance until after she had been away for two nights. Why was that?'

'I thought she would come back.'

'Are you sure you didn't report her missing out of a misplaced sense of pride? You didn't want people to look on you as a man whose wife had walked out on him?'

'No.'

'Or that you won't confess to knowing your wife had a lover because it would make you appear a cuckold?'

Deadly Pattern

Burton appeared genuinely outraged and distressed. It satisfied Masters. He had hoped to get a reaction. This, he thought, was the genuine article. He was prepared to believe Burton had no knowledge of any other man in his wife's life.

'Right, Mr Burton. Then why the delay in reporting her missing?'

'I just don't know.' Burton spread his hands. 'I wish to God I'd done it straight away, but . . .'

'One always clings to hopes?'

'Yes, I suppose so.'

'Were you cross with your wife for leaving you?'

'At first. It was only later that I got seriously worried. Then I rang the police.'

'Thank you, Mr Burton. I think I can understand your state of mind, even if I deplore your procrastination.' He got up and stared through the french windows at the bare flower beds. The spikes of some bulbs were showing through strongly. But little else. He felt even more depressed.

The children came back. Beryl said: 'It was covered in dust. Nobody's done anything to that room since Mum went.' She put the dress-box on the table and lifted the lid. A jumble of snaps and more formal photographs lay haphazard in the bottom tray.

After Burton had looked at each photograph, he set it aside for Masters. Hill joined the Chief Inspector and looked over his shoulder. Burton worked through conscientiously, jotting down names occasionally, but a cardboard tube containing a panoramic photograph he put on one side without examination. Masters said: 'Not this one?'

'Hardly. It's a photograph of the whole school when Frances was a girl. There's about three hundred people on it. I can't go through that lot and remember the names.'

'Perhaps not.' Masters drew the long photograph from the tube. To keep it opened out, he had to hold one end, Hill the other. The caption read: 'Finstoft Grammar School for Girls 1945'. Three hundred of them, as Burton had said, arranged in tiers along one side of the school quad. On the front row, in chairs, mistresses in gowns, many in spectacles, with—by now—severely old-fashioned hair-do's. Hill seemed amused. He pointed out the inevitable oddities—the fat, the roguish, the squinting, and then he said: 'Aye, aye. They even did it in those days, did they?'

'Did what?'

'See this lass, chief?' He pointed to a girl with a smirking face at his end of the photograph. 'Look at the one at your end.'

Masters looked carefully. 'The same girl.'

'That's right. The camera traverses slowly from left to right to get the whole lot in. If it didn't, they'd have to plant it so far away that the faces would be indistinguishable in the photograph. Somebody pretty nippy like this girl looks to have been, could be standing at the starting end, then when the lens had passed her she could dodge along behind the back row and reach the other end before the camera. That's what this girl did. Great fun, being on one photograph twice. But I bet she got it in the neck when the thing was developed and the headmistress saw it.'

Burton looked up. 'What's that?'

'Some girl up to the old dodge of appearing twice on the same panorama,' said Masters.

'Oh, yes. Mary Starkey. I'd better put her down. I never knew her, but I've heard Frances speak about her when she's been showing the kids these photographs in the past.'

Beryl said: 'Mum always said she was the naughtiest girl in the school. She was in Mum's form and used to whistle at boys from the cloakroom window.'

'She looks a bit of a tearaway, here,' Hill observed.

Masters rolled up the photograph. He picked up a snap of Connie Mace and examined it carefully. Hill, riffling through, came up with a photograph of three girls in black bathing costumes and white rubber caps. They were one-piece swimsuits, with little legs and wide straps over the shoulders. The three young faces—and even the immature bodies—looked self-conscious. Hill looked at it for a moment and said: 'Here she is again. That Starkey girl, isn't it?'

Burton glanced at it. 'Oh yes. It was taken at the bathing pool. That's Frances in the middle. Mary Starkey on her left and Robina Judge on her right.'

There was silence as they all returned to work. Robert said: 'Shall we put in the milkman?' Masters nodded and said: 'Try to put in everybody, but say who they are in brackets if you can.'

When the lists were finished, Masters gathered them up. Burton said: 'By God, you're thorough. The locals didn't go to all this trouble.'

'Aren't you thorough in your profession or business, Mr Burton?' Masters inquired.

Deadly Pattern

'Of course.'

'This is my profession, remember. By the way, what do you do?'

'Me? I'm a fish merchant on Hawksfleet docks.'

'Fish *merchant*?'

'Wholesale.'

'I see.'

'I buy on the market and supply customers all over the country. It's a good life. Cold and wet sometimes, but active.'

Masters thanked Burton and asked if Hill could use the telephone to call Green. Burton said: 'By all means. But won't you stay for a cup of tea? Beryl will soon make us one.'

'I'd like that.' Masters turned to Hill: 'Tell Inspector Green we'll be with him in half an hour, and if Mr Burton doesn't object, fetch in P.C. Garner for a cup of tea.'

*

Inspector Green and Sergeant Brant knocked on the door of 'Thrums'. It was opened by a young man in his early twenties. Green eyed him closely. The youth was obviously extremely careful of his appearance. His grey trousers were well creased; the brown and fawn check sports jacket spotlessly clean; the pale blue shirt and club tie immaculate; the ginger hair carefully parted and brushed. But Green didn't like the face. Too podgy by half, with too little colour, too many freckles, and eyes that were too small for the vast expanse of flesh. Green thought he looked supercilious, and this, for Green, was more than enough to arouse instant dislike. In Green's view, Masters was supercilious, and this had done nothing to endear him to the type.

'I'd like to see Mr Osborn, please,' said Green.

'Who would?'

Swallowing hard, Green said: 'That's right. You can't be too careful with callers these days.' Then raising his voice to give it an edge of menace: 'I'm from Scotland Yard. The name is Green. Inspector Green.'

'Wait. I'll ask Dad if he'll see you.' He disappeared.

Brant said airily: 'Nice chap. Nobody likes him.'

It was Osborn himself who came next to the door. 'I'm Frank Osborn. My son tells me you want to see me.'

'That's the idea. Now, sir, if you would allow us in . . .'

Osborn opened the door and stepped aside. He was putting on flesh too early. A gross man. Heavily dark in the beard area. Flesh puffed up round small eyes. Coarse red mouth. A figure that gave his waistcoat a bow front and trousers that had to be cut too large round the seat for their length. His hair, still black, was oiled into place and waved vertically at the sides. Green thought to himself that it was funny how often really dark parents produced ginger kids. A freak of nature he'd met more than once.

The house gave an appearance of wealth. The hall was big and square with oak block flooring and white, long-haired rugs; the staircase wide, painted cream and carpeted in Turkey red. The doors were heavy, with polished copper knobs and finger plates. Almost automatically Green found himself treading gingerly as he followed Osborn into a sitting-room with an Indian carpet and suite in matching chintz. Osborn said to his son who was standing with his back to the fire: 'You can go, Berry.'

'If you don't mind, I would like your son to stay,' Green said.

'And I wouldn't.'

'Have it your way.' He turned to Brant. 'Take young Mr Osborn to the station and question him there.'

'Don't play the heavy with me, Inspector,' said Osborn.

'I'm investigating a murder, Mr Osborn. Not one murder. Five. Now let me put you right about a few things. I've no need to come the heavy with anyone, because I can get a free hand in a case as important as this from everybody from the Home Secretary downwards. If I as much as whisper that anybody—by as much as a flicker of an eyelid—is trying to obstruct me in the execution of my duty, I'll get a warrant for arrest on reasonable suspicion without having to ask for it. Now I don't want to go that far, because it'd be a waste of my time. That's why I've come to see you here in your house, rather than call you into the local station. But don't try to twist my arm, Mr Osborn. I've seen too many like you crawling out of the woodwork to be very impressed.'

'So that's the way you want to play it. Well, let me tell you, Inspector . . .'

'No. Let me tell you. I'll play it any way you like. But I came here to get some information and I'm going to get it. Now.'

'I don't like the way you're going about it.'

'And I don't like the way you've received me. So now we've both said what we think, shall we sit down?'

Green sat on the settee, sharing it with Brant who had his notebook ready. The Osborns, father and son, sat in wing chairs flanking the

Deadly Pattern

fireplace. Osborn lit a cigar without offering them round. Green said: 'Besides Mr Bertram here, you have a daughter, Mr Osborn.'

'Julia. She isn't in. She's out shopping.'

'Pity. I shall want to see her.'

'She'll be back.' It was a sneer.

'Right. Mrs Osborn disappeared on the twenty-eighth of January. That was a Tuesday. Evening. Now, let's see where everybody was at the time.'

'We've already given this to the local police.'

'So you have. I've read it. It was your firm's annual party. You were there.' He looked hard at Osborn. 'A pretty bald sort of statement. Takes up two lines of a notebook. By the time I've finished it'll fill the *Sunday Times*. So start talking.'

'I'm chairman of my own firm,' Osborn began.

'Which is?'

'A fish curing company on the Hawksfleet docks—Frank Osborn and Son. We freeze fish, too, in over-the-counter packs.'

'You give your employees an annual party?'

'Yes.'

'What does it cost?'

Berry said: 'We don't *give* the party. The firm has a social club to which everybody contributes. The employees run their own party and we chip in to make up the cost. This year we gave a hundred and fifty pounds. Two pounds for every employee.'

'Generous of you. Where was this party held?'

'Where it's always held. At the Hawksfleet Town Hall.'

'You went?'

'Of course. I'm the chairman, aren't I? The workers expect to see their bosses there.'

To the left-inclined Green this was typical of all that he hated in capitalism. However, he kept his voice even. 'It was a mixed party?'

'Of course it was mixed. We employ both sexes.'

'Seventy-five men and women, evenly mixed.'

'A hundred and fifty,' said Berry. 'They were each allowed one partner. That's why we gave two quid a head.'

'I see.' Green turned to Osborn. 'Then in that case, as you were getting matey with the workers, and sharing their party, why didn't Mrs Osborn go with you?'

'My wife was ill.'

'What with?'

'Headache.'

'Let's make it quite clear that I can't accept that explanation.'

'And why not?'

'Because you know as well as I do that any headache in the world can be cured inside half an hour with today's drugs. And as the boss's wife, Mrs Osborn must have known that her presence at this party was a bit of vital P.R. work which no wise boss would forgo for the price of a packet of pills. So now, why didn't Mrs Osborn go to the party?'

'She was ill, I tell you.'

'Too seriously to attend the party?'

'Yes.'

'But not seriously enough to call in a doctor?'

'I don't know.'

'Did you ask her?'

'No.'

'So your wife was too ill to go with you on what any normal boss would consider a duty engagement, and yet you didn't try to find out what the trouble was that was losing you valuable P.R. with your workers.'

'It was an indefinite illness.'

'Starting when?'

'I don't know. Women get these things.'

'Had she complained of it before?'

'I don't know.'

'So your wife may have had a long-standing illness which you didn't seek advice about.'

'What are you getting at?'

'The truth, I hope. And trying to find the relationship you enjoyed with your wife. Now, when did this illness come on?'

Berry said: 'She started complaining on the Sunday.'

'Thank you. What did you do about it?'

'Nothing. I met her in the hall. She'd been on the phone. I was just going out. She looked a bit white, so I asked her if she felt all right. She said she did, but she was a bit headachy and I wasn't to worry. So I went.'

'Could the phone call have upset her?'

'I dunno. I don't know who it was from.'

'Right. Any signs of this headache earlier?'

'No. Not that I know of.'

'You, Mr Osborn?'

'No.'

'Then in that case, can you tell me when she called off the party?' asked Green.

'Oh, sometime that Tuesday evening.'

'You can't remember exactly when?'

'No. How could I?'

'By remembering what steps you took to see she was all right, to cure her, to persuade her to accompany you.'

'I can't remember.'

'You did none of those things?'

'I may have done.'

'Which suggests you didn't. Perhaps you weren't too keen that she should accompany you.'

'You've just now said I would have been keen because of her P.R. value. Remember?'

'But you negatived that, Mr Osborn. And as you can't remember urging her to join you I'll assume you didn't. In which case I want to know why.'

'By God, I'll . . .'

'What?'

Osborn didn't reply. Green changed the subject. 'What was Mrs Osborn wearing when she went out?'

Berry said: 'Julia found out what was missing. A top coat and one of those furry caps. A white one, with gloves to match and a purse.'

'So it seems she dressed and went of her own free will.'

'Looks like it.'

'A sick woman, too ill to accompany her husband, but not too ill to take herself off somewhere else on a cold January night. Doesn't make sense, does it?'

'Nothing makes blasted sense,' said Osborn.

'It does to me. I'm definitely of the opinion Mrs Osborn was not ill. If she had been—for more than two days—she'd have called the doctor. I believe she had no wish to accompany you, Mr Osborn. For one of two reasons. Because she had another engagement she didn't want to tell you about, or because you didn't particularly want her with you. And as you got quite threatening a moment ago, I'll guess at the latter. Tell me why she wouldn't go with you.'

'Go to hell.'

'No doubt I will—eventually. But if you won't tell me, I'll have to make the obvious assumption and follow that up.'

'What assumption?'

'That you've another woman in tow.'

'You're raving.'

'It shouldn't take me more than ten minutes among your work people on Monday morning to see whether I'm right or wrong. You've seen for yourself how tenacious I can be and what wonderful assumptions I can arrive at from the answers I'm given.'

'Better tell him, Dad,' said Berry.

'Tell him, you bloody fool? Tell him what?'

'About Lindy Vicary.'

'Shut up.'

'*Miss* Lindy Vicary? Or *Mrs*?'

Osborn threw his cigar stub into the fire. 'He doesn't know what he's talking about, the young fool. Lindy Vicary's my secretary. A single girl.'

'Did she take a partner to the party?'

Berry glanced at Green and shook his head.

'I see. So *you* were free, Mr Osborn, and *Miss Vicary* was free. Very convenient. Did your wife know of the affair?'

'What affair?'

'Between you and Miss Vicary.'

'There is no affair.'

'I'm sorry. In a case like this I can't take your word for it.'

Berry said: 'Look, Dad. You'll be getting yourself in deep. I'm sick and fed up of the remarks I hear on the docks about you knocking off Lindy on the side. Everybody knows. The husbands of all Mother's friends know. Don't you think they'll have had a good laugh over it at home? Don't you think some pussy'll have made it her business to tell Mother—and enjoyed doing it? Well? Don't you? And who d'you think's going to keep quiet about the fact that you were missing from the party for over an hour that night? When they wanted you to present the dance prizes you couldn't be found—until somebody had the bright idea of going to the car park and dragging you off Lindy who, according to rumour—and I believe it—was more than half undressed in the back of your Jag.' Osborn glowered at his son, gritting his teeth, his cheeks red with anger.

'There you are, then, Mr Osborn,' said Green. 'If you'd told me first off about this bit of frippet I'd have understood straight away and we'd have saved ourselves a bit of time. Now, how long were you with this woman?'

Osborn was sulky. 'All the time.'

'That, at least, I can believe. And you see where that gets you, for the moment at any rate. It clears you of murdering your wife.'

'What? Good God, man, you don't think I killed Joanna?'

'We're suspicious of everybody, Mr Osborn. And most women who're murdered are killed by either a husband or lover.'

'It's ridiculous. If I'd killed Joanna, it would mean I'd killed three or four other women.'

'That's right. So let's try and eliminate them, too, shall we? D'you keep a diary?'

'No.'

'Pity. Now these dates—Friday, January the tenth—remember it?'

'No.'

'Wednesday the fifteenth.'

'No.'

Berry said: 'I do. Dad and I were in London.'

'Doing what, Mr Berry?'

'The White Fish Industry meeting. Curing Division. Dad goes as the firm's chairman. I go as secretary. We went down on Tuesday by the midday train and came back on Friday afternoon. On the Wednesday evening we attended the president's cocktail party.'

'Fair enough. No more questions about that. But there's something I want you both to do for me.'

'What's that?'

'Try to think if Mrs Osborn was in any way connected with Mrs Burton, Mrs Severn, Mrs Pogson or Mrs Baker.'

'She knew them all, slightly. They were all reported missing before she was, and she said so.'

'But none of them was a close friend of hers?'

'Not that I know of.'

'Right, then I'll have to ask you to write down who her friends and acquaintances were. Mr Berry, you make a list of her recent contacts. Mr Osborn, you think back right to the time when you first knew your wife and jot down every name you can remember. Any old photographs you've got might help.'

Osborn took out a gold propelling pencil. He was now more co-operative. He said: 'Berry, get that old album of your mother's . . .' The telephone rang in the hall. 'And answer that.'

Berry poked his head round the door. He said to Green: 'It's a Sergeant Hill, for you.'

Chapter Four

In the car on the way back to the Estuary, nobody spoke anything more than brief intermittent sentences. It was dark, and Finstoft had again settled down, after its afternoon of activity, to a night of suspended animation. The shops had closed their doors, but the internal lighting gave them snatches of 3–D pictures as the car drove past. It was as cheerless as a theatre after the comedy has finished and all but the pilot lights have been extinguished. But in this case, not even the atmosphere of laughter remained.

'One quick drink when we get in,' said Masters. 'Then P.C. Garner can go, and the rest of us will confer in my room before dinner. I hope that will leave us free for an hour or so later.'

Green said: 'Seems the best plan. I didn't even get a cup of tea out of the Osborns. Mean as muck, they were. And twice as nasty.'

The Sundowner was almost empty as they trooped down the stairs. Sitting on the same stool as the night before was Derek Tintern. He was arguing with Shirl about the change she had given him. He said: 'I gave you a pound note. No. Ten shillings?'

Shirl said emphatically: 'It was a pound, ducky. I'm not out to do you.'

'A pound, yes. You say you're not out to do me. But you *are* doing me. A double gin is . . . what is a double gin? Anyhow, I think you've charged me for a tonic.'

'Feel for the bedpost, love. Double gin's five an' four. If you'd got a tonic an' all, it'd have been *six* an' four. Now look at your change.' She counted as he held it out on his palm. 'Two an' six, four an' six, an' tuppence is four an' eight. Four an' eight an' five an' four is ten bob. An' ten makes a pound.'

Tintern looked morose and kept the money in his hand, without leaving a tip in the ashtray. Masters noticed he appeared to be wearing the same shirt as the night before, but now, on the right collar front was an ink smudge. He thought Tintern must be one of those who put a clean shirt on each evening, and then wear it again the following day. It meant Tintern hadn't yet been upstairs to wash and change. Masters felt Sherlock Holmesish about his deduction.

Shirl moved down the counter towards them. Brant said: 'Having a bit of trouble?'

'With him? No. He often does it. I've never understood why he can't add up the change for a pound right, when after dinner he can play bridge like a champion an' never miscount a point. He's good at it, you know. All the old bags who play think he's marvellous.'

'There's nowt as queer as fowk,' said Brant. 'Four pints of draught Worthington, please, Shirl. No! Five. I was forgetting P.C. Garner.'

Two or three more people clattered down the stairs. Shirl said: 'Looks like we'll be filling up a bit more tonight than we have done this last week. It's you people who've done it.'

'What? Five of us? That's not many in a bar on a Saturday night. Fifty, yes!' exclaimed Green.

'Oh, I didn't mean yourselves, love. I meant the bit in the paper tonight. Given 'em a bit of confidence to go out in the dark again, I suppose.'

Hill said: 'So we've hit the headlines in the local rag, have we? Got a copy we can have a look at?'

She leaned slightly forward, without looking down, to feel for the paper under the bar. Green said to Brant in a whisper: 'Just look at that. I can see her belly button.'

The *Hawksfleet Evening Courier* had majored on the presence of the team from Scotland Yard. Old cases had been dredged up and presented in potted versions. Even photographs from months before had been reprinted. There was nothing new, but Masters, his egotism almost showing, said: 'I'd like a copy of this.'

'Keep it, love. It'll go well in your album.'

Green sniggered. 'Press-cuttings book, please. Bound in soft leather with gilt edges. Of vital historic importance in the annals of crime.'

Shirl said: 'An' why not? I'd let him invite me up to show it to me any time.' With a coquettish flick of the head she moved away to serve more customers.

Masters said good humouredly: 'A friend at last,' and glanced after her. Hill, looking the same way, said: 'That chap's still not satisfied with his change. Look, he's got it on the bar, counting it.' Masters looked. Tintern, moving the coins about, like chessmen, with one long, bony forefinger. Green said: 'He looks like my missus counting up to see if she can afford a new pair of nylons after she's paid the milkman on a Saturday.' He put down his tankard. 'Well, if that's it, I've had it.'

*

In Masters's room, Green made his report. He told very fully of his interview with Osborn and the discovery of the Vicary skeleton in the cupboard.

'Did you see the daughter?' Masters asked.

'No. She hadn't returned when we came away.'

'Did they express any worry about her not being back? After all, it's less than a month since her mother disappeared.'

'That shower? They haven't a thought for anybody but themselves, except perhaps the old man for his bit of capurtle, and Berry boy for his own image on the docks.'

'What about that phone call on Sunday? You say her son said she looked white and ill after it. Could it have been blackmail?' Hill asked.

'Now don't start bringing the black into it. We've got enough on our plates already,' said Green.

Hill said: 'I know. But from what you learned, and we learned, this afternoon, these women went out of their own free will, but without telling anybody. To me that sounds as if the black was being put on. Who'd lure them out like that better than a blackmailer? And when you mentioned that phone call making her ill . . .'

'There's a point there,' Masters agreed. 'It's as well you brought it up, but I don't think we'll consider it for several reasons. First, as Inspector Green said, it would complicate things. Second—and this is a more practical reason—is any blackmailer likely to have a hold over *five* women, all of the same age and type and all living in the same district? The person who gets blackmailed is usually a man—like Osborn—who doesn't want his wife to know he's been unfaithful. And the third point is this. A blackmailer rarely kills off the goose that lays the golden eggs; and for our man to kill off five laying geese seems so unlikely to me that I'm going to discount it from the beginning.'

'Put like that, it does seem to rule out blackmail. But what's the explanation of that phone call that upset her?'

'It could have been anything,' said Green.

'At a guess I'd say her son put his finger on it when he said some pussy would tell her about her husband's affair with this Lindy woman,' Masters said. 'What about an anonymous call, say? Mightn't that upset her? Make her refuse to go with him to the party where she knew the other woman would be, with everybody present knowing just what the score was? I reckon it would. Any woman with a hide thinner than a battle-cruiser's would shrink from entering those particular waters.'

Green said: 'That sounds fair enough. And that Joanna dame—from the pictures I saw—was quite a thin-skinned dish. But the skin was all beauty. She'd got those big, round eyes like half-sucked acid drops, and I can tell you that in a low-cut evening gown she wasn't one of your tennis-ball-in-sock types. She couldn't half chuck a chest.'

Masters filled his pipe. 'Our Mrs Burton seemed to have faded a bit. She wasn't bad as a girl, but I got the impression that she was the sort who, once she'd got a husband and family, let herself go. The sort that liked playing houses. The born housewife—in its less glamorous sense. And talking of photographs, what about the list of names?'

'Thirty-two,' said Green. 'It didn't strike me that Osborn and Son were very knowledgeable about—or interested in—Joanna's pals.'

'They couldn't have been. We got over a hundred names,' said Hill.

'Clever boy.'

'We were lucky,' said Masters. 'We had the whole family there, and it may be that Mrs Burton was more gregarious than Mrs Osborn. But even so, I can't believe that a woman can live for forty odd years in the same area without being acquainted with more than thirty-two people. I think you'd better see the daughter when you can, and get her to contribute her mite.'

'Tomorrow?'

'I don't see why not. She can't go shopping on Sundays. And it'll even up the jobs. Between us we've got three more families to see. You do one of those and Julia. I'll do the other two.' He turned to Hill and Brant. 'I'd like you two to compare lists. Sort out anybody who figures on both.'

*

Saturday night was obviously the night the residents of Finstoft—or at least those who could afford it—dined out. Masters and his party had some difficulty in finding a table. They were left standing by the dining-room door while the head waiter beat the bounds of the room, tails agitated, right hand held high ready to snap finger and thumb should the need arise. To the surprise of the others, Masters didn't appear to be as put out because his table hadn't been reserved as they had expected him to be. The reason was apparent after about twenty seconds. As they stood waiting, first one

Deadly Pattern

pair of eyes, then another, turned towards them. A surreptitious nudge here, and a quiet word there spread the news. People sitting with backs to them turned. Masters, towering above his three big consorts, in his freshly valeted new suit, was enjoying himself. He had the confidence of knowing that he looked well, and that his reputation was something of a byword even here in Finstoft. He was indulging himself, and giving the diners a good view for their money.

Then they were ushered away, to a table for six from which a reserved label had been moved. Some other party would have to wait. Masters in high humour ordered smoked trout, devilled kidneys and crêpes suzette. With a bottle of hock. He didn't care for red wines, and drank white even when the blood followed the knife. He was more than scornful of drink know-alls who practised what they preached even against their own palates.

Green ate stewed oxtail. He said to Hill: 'Good grub, this. Better than those terrine things and whatnot.'

'If you can get anything off the bones.'

'It's as messy to eat as spaghetti,' said Brant.

'Quite right,' said Masters, tackling the three flattened spheres of kidney spread across his plate. 'To eat oxtail and spag bol properly, you've got to be stripped to the waist in a soundproof booth.'

Green said: 'In that case they're the right dishes for mixed parties.' He pushed a cotton-bobbin bone to the edge of his plate. It fell off and dirtied the tablecloth. He swore under his breath, and made even more of a mess trying to retrieve it.

The dining-room was beginning to empty as they left the table. Green said: 'Anybody for a snifter?'

'Some' of us have work to do. Those lists,' Hill said.

'So've I,' added Masters.

'What?'

'I want to look at your survey work.'

'Oh, come on. Just for a snort.'

Masters knew that for all Green's bounce, he would probably fight shy of going down alone to the Sundowner, to a room full of strangers whom he would probably regard—without knowing them—as the parasites of society. There was this sense of inadequacy in Green at all social gatherings not directly connected with his work. Masters decided the civil thing would be to go along with him. The two of them descended the stairs to the bar, but had difficulty in actually entering the room. They stood, peering over the heads of groups, wondering how to reach the bar or a vacant floor space, when above the din they heard a cry. Looking over to the corner where they had been sitting the previous evening, Masters saw Swaine. The little doctor was standing on the upholstered wall-bench in order to see above the intervening bodies. He was signalling them to join him.

They pushed through the crowd. Swaine said: 'Thought you were never coming. You must have had your nosebags on for two hours. Looked in at the dining-room. There you were, champing away, and I thought that at the rate you were going you'd be out faster than colleague Bannister did his mile. Not a bit of it. I've been guarding this corner at risk of this an' that for an hour or more.' He looked round, and saw one of the waiters imported to help Shirl at a nearby table. 'Hi! Sid. Two pints of Worthington and a strong ale twice.' He turned to Masters. 'Well, what news?'

'Very little to give you. Something to ask you. The necks of the victims. No scratch marks?'

'Nary a one. It nearly made a whore's drawers of my investigation, I can tell you. I read it up, you know, just to make sure. And there should be scratches.'

'Or bruises?'

'In place of the scratches, yes. Of course there are the bruises caused by the strangler's hands, just where I'd expect them to be, but none caused by the victims while struggling to release themselves.'

'And they definitely weren't dead when strangled?' said Green.

'Not a bit of it. I can assure you they were alive up to the time occlusion of the windpipe caused death.'

'And they weren't struck down or drugged?'

'Definitely not.'

'Nor their arms tied?'

'Not a sign of a cord anywhere. As there would have been if they *had* been tied. Tight ropes would themselves have made marks, and looser bonds would have cut into the flesh of anybody struggling against them.'

'It's a real porridge,' said Masters.

'I'm delighted to hear you say so. Not because I don't want you to succeed, but because I've been so bloody puzzled myself.'

'Yet you didn't mention this last night.'

'Neither did you. I wanted to hear your unprompted reactions.'

Masters said: 'Then how's this? Pressure on the carotid arteries would stop the blood flow to the brain, wouldn't it?'

'Most certainly.' He looked up as the waiter approached and paid him. 'Thanks, Sid. Missus and kids over the flu yet?'

'Going along nicely, Doctor, thank you.'

'That's the ticket. Take your wife a nip home with you. It'll do her the world of good.'

The waiter promised to do so, and turned away to take more orders. Swaine said: 'Cheers, gentlemen. Now where were we?'

'Carotid arteries.'

'Oh yes. Stop the flow and you'd knock them out in a dead faint all right.'

'There you are, then,' said Green.

'No, you're not there. I can't tell you exactly how long the human brain can do without blood, because I've never experimented. And neither has anybody else. But I can tell you that the period will vary between different people.'

'Within what bracket?'

'I should say between twenty seconds in somebody old and frail and already suffering from partial cerebrovascular disease to as long as perhaps three minutes in a healthy person. And those women were good specimens. Most of us are, at forty, in spite of the beliefs of modern youth.'

'So it might take longer to knock them out that way than to strangle them?' Green asked.

'It might, easily. But there are bigger snags than that. First of all the killer would have to find the carotids on both sides. Exactly, mind you. And that's not easy. Then the depression would have left two bruises—one each side. And there weren't any such bruises. And lastly, if he'd adopted that method there'd have been the same longitudinal scratching or bruising as for strangulation. The victim would try—with almost unlimited strength at such a time—to wrench away the killer's hands. So I can assure you the carotids were not occluded.'

Green said 'Thanks' dryly, and picked up his tankard. Masters said: 'Well, he managed it somehow, and we've got to find out how.'

Swaine raised his glass: 'Good luck! You'll need it.'

They talked together until time was called. Swaine left, and Masters with Green crossed the foyer. As they passed the card room, through the glass door, they caught a glimpse of Tintern playing an elderly man at chess. Masters paused for a moment. He said to Green: 'Our friend's winning.'

Green said, moving on: 'I've never played chess.'

'I get no time for it,' said Masters. 'All I ever do is the chess problems in the papers. Which is Hill's room?'

Green led him to the room where the two sergeants, in shirt sleeves, were working at the lists of names. Papers in different scrawls covered the bed. Masters knew the answer before he asked the question: 'Any luck?'

Hill said: 'Not a skerrick. Sorry.'

'Nothing at all?'

'Well, they both know people called Smith—as you would expect. But not the same ones. And they both know a Harrison. But they're not the same person either. One's a male, one a female.'

'Those five women must have had some common contacts,' said Masters. 'They've lived round here for forty years and moved in the same circles. Mrs Osborn and Mrs Burton went to the same school, didn't they?'

'Same school. Two years between them. And Osborn told me his missus had remarked before her own disappearance that she was acquainted with all the others,' Green said.

'That's what I'd have thought.'

Brant said: 'The only other overlap is among Christian names. There are about half a dozen Johns, three Marys, and several pairs of the more common monnikers.'

'Bear them in mind. Computerize them in your old heads, and when we get the rest, we'll see what you can come up with.'

Masters went alone to his own room. The large scale map they had used in the morning was crumpled and folded against its original creases. He went down on his knees and spread it on the floor, smoothing it with his hands. It was a sorry mess. Bullimore's original crosses, large and straggling, with the victims' names written alongside, were overlapped by Green's much neater, but profuse work. The original rays were drawn in, the bearing and distance lines, the new locations. All this on top of the features already printed on it made the area look like a child's scribbling pad. Masters gazed at it for some minutes, seeking inspiration. Then, because his knees were sore, he got up and paced the room, filling his pipe, and frowning in thought. When the Warlock Flake was burning gently, he removed his jacket, slung it on the bed, and sat back in the armchair. His brain would not click over. He was trying to force it uphill to a peak which he knew was there but could not recognize. He felt if he could get over this hump he could freewheel down the other side. He tried logical thought. What was he looking for? He had to admit to himself he didn't know. Was what he was attempting to do, useful? Did it matter that Bullimore had made a near guess at the locations of the graves? He had to admit that he'd never before known the need to pinpoint the location of a body to the nearest yard. These four made the corners of a four-sided box. An irregular box. Shaped a bit like a kite. But he remembered enough of his geometry to know that any four dots, made haphazardly on a piece of paper and then joined up, enclosed an irregular box. He got to his feet, and with his propelling pencil and the back of an envelope from his jacket pocket, experimented. No matter what he did, he got one of two or three shapes—rectangle, diamond or kite—all recognizably within each category, even though flattened or squashed or elongated.

He sat down again. A clock somewhere struck midnight, the chimes distorted by the wind which, in the stillness of the night, could still be heard gusting round the buildings.

Peeved by his lack of success, he picked up the map, and folded it yet again, flattening the new creases with his fine, slim fingers. Fingers which were so obviously the end product of generations of forbears who had never performed manual labour that they irritated Green. With just the relevant square foot or so of plan before him, Masters leaned back in his chair and gazed. No inspiration came. He cursed Bullimore for using a liquid pencil that couldn't be rubbed out. Green at least had used pencil, and though his marks were no hair-lines, at least they could be rubbed out.

Rubbed out! Like those poor, unsuspecting women, who had gone. . . . He pulled himself together. His mind was wandering because of lack of sleep after a heavy day and through trying to cope with the problems of a new and difficult case before the previous one could be said to have been fairly completed. However, 'rubbed out' remained. He took the cap from the top of his propelling pencil. He used the small, red, cylindrical eraser on the lines drawn in by Green. Carefully. So as not to destroy the actual map spots of the graves. Fussily, he brushed away the dirty grey detritus, and again sat back to gaze at the plan. No inspiration.

He sat for ten minutes before getting up again to take the six-inch plastic ruler from his jacket pocket. The last time he had used this was for measuring the depth of a gunshot outlet wound. It had stirred clotted gore, and though well washed afterwards, he fancied he could still see dark brown stains remaining in the black measurement marks. Carefully, holding the pencil loosely so that it followed the ruler of its own free will, he stroked in faint new lines across the roughened surface. Green's locations were marked by dots in little circles. He joined them up. Kite shape again. He decided he would join each one to every other one in turn. Then his tired brain realized that this would mean only two more lines— the diagonals which would represent the framework canes of the kite he'd had as a child. He completed his task. He was no further forward. He took up the rubber again and started to remove what he had done. The rubber was too small to allow him great sweeps across the map to obliterate his useless handiwork. He had to take it line by line, longitudinally. The lopsided box first. With the edge of his little finger he brushed away the clinging crumbs of rubber, flicking the surface of the paper clean.

He stopped in mid stroke.

The diagonals remained. They made a perfect cross. Long stem and short stem, cutting exactly at right angles.

Something stirred in his mind. What was it? Just at one corner he hadn't quite erased the box outline. It was there. A little dunce's cap; an apex at the top of the long stem. An arrow-head.

His brain regathered a little energy. An arrow-head like those used for denoting north on a map. But this one pointed . . . where did it point? . . . he opened the sheet frenziedly to compare it with the printed north indicator . . . this one pointed east. Due east.

A cross pointing due east!

He remembered the head and foot markers in the four graves. Green had said the bodies had lain east and west. Heads to the east.

It must mean something. He peered closely at his work. The two stems of the cross intersected on the square, black blob of a bungalow. Then the idea came to him. The fifth body! Bullimore's men had probed the open foreshore and dunes. Had they probed underneath these bungalows, each sitting above the ground on its bobbins of piles? Masters knew instinctively that they hadn't. There were hundreds of bungalows. Many days' work for many men. And the other bodies had been found in the open. No reason to search under bungalows.

But he now felt certain he knew where the fifth body was. Could pinpoint it. Symbolism . . . patterns . . . He pulled himself together. He was dropping off in the chair. With reluctant heaviness he moved over to the washbasin and swilled his face in cold water: cleaned his teeth against the foul taste of strong, stale tobacco: and undressed.

He slept this night without a vestige of a dream to trouble him.

*

At breakfast the next morning Green was grumbling. 'Here we are. First down. Nobody else in the dining-room. All lying in except us.'

'What about the waiters?' said Hill.

Two rather bored young men and two rather older women were standing waiting to serve the host that hadn't yet appeared. Every so often one of them looked across at the four policemen, not, apparently, to see if there was anything required on the table, but because they were the subject of the desultory conversation. Green, out of sheer cussedness waved a hand. When the waiter came Green said he didn't like the chunks in Oxford marmalade, could he have some Golden Shred.

Brant said to Masters: 'What's the form this morning? Shall we go to the Osborns first and then on to one of the other three?'

'No. We'll do that this afternoon.' He got no further with his explanation, because Tintern walked in and stopped at the door to complain that his morning tea had been late, and so he was late for breakfast. The conversation was audible in the quiet room. One of the waiters said: 'It's Sunday morning, Mr Tintern. An extra half hour in bed won't do you any harm.'

'I must be on time. I don't like being late.'

'Never mind, sir. It's a day of rest. Now, how about a nice dish of ham and eggs to start you off properly?'

'Ham and eggs to start me off? No. Grapefruit juice and toast only, please. And I'd like it straightaway or I shall be even later.'

Hill said quietly: 'It's just too bad about him.'

'He looks a bit rough to me,' said Brant.

'Hectic game of chess last night. He's exhausted,' said Green. Masters was noticing that Tintern was again wearing the shirt with the ink-smudged collar and reflecting wryly that his Holmesian theory of the night before had been all wrong.

Tintern sat down a few tables away without a glance in their direction. The waiter hurried over to him with a glass of grapefruit juice and a rack of toast. 'Here we are, sir. You get that down pretty nippy like, and you'll find you've made up for lost time.'

'I've lost my time maid,' Tintern said.

The waiter stared for a moment and then laughed: 'Oh, yes, sir. She didn't come—the chambermaid—on time, did she? Pity that. I'll have a word at the office, sir.'

Green said: 'Some sense of humour! If I couldn't crack a better joke than that, even at this time on a Sunday morning, I'd keep quiet. He's lost his time maid, indeed. If she was anything like mine she needed losing.'

'I'm in a bit of a hurry myself, so if you'd not mind pushing along . . .' said Masters.

'What's up? Our interviewees won't have opened their little eyes yet.'

'We're going to the dunes.'

'Again? What the hell for?'

'To dig up Mrs Barbara Severn.'

'Oh no! The locals can do that. You're not getting me digging up corpses a month . . .' Green stopped, and stared at Masters: 'You what? What did you say? Severn? Severn? She's the one who hasn't been found.'

'She has now. I know where she is.'

Green looked sceptical, but he'd had enough experience of Masters to know that he never made claims such as this without justification. Of course, Green was thinking, he'll slip up some day and I'll have the laugh on him, but the bastard seems mighty sure of himself this time.

As if divining Green's thoughts, Masters said: 'The earlier we're out there, the better. It's Sunday, remember, and there may well be a rubbernecking crowd later on. I don't want them there when we produce the body.'

'If you're so sure, are you taking Dr Swaine with you?'

'I prefer to do what we have to do in private. Swaine can take over later.'

Brant and Hill had said nothing. They were wondering how Masters had managed to guess where the fifth body would be lying, but they were too wise to question his ability to find it.

*

As they left the hotel, Masters glanced up. The sky looked like a slab of dough kneaded with dirty fingers—pasty white with grey streaks. A lovely day for an exhumation.

P.C. Garner, standing on the pavement, said: 'Morning, sir. The Super's here.'

Bullimore was just getting out of the car which had pulled up behind the Vauxhall. He called: 'Wanted to catch you before you went off. Just to hear if there's any news or anything I can do to help.'

'You can help. You timed your arrival nicely,' said Masters.
'Good. What d'you want?'
'Help.'
'What with?'
'Exhuming Mrs Severn.'
Bullimore stared for a moment. 'You've found her?'
'Shall we say, located her? We're just off to prove my theory.'
'Or disprove it,' said Green.
Bullimore ignored Green. 'Are you trying to tell me that never having been near this place before yesterday, and sitting in a hotel miles away from the site, you can deduce where a woman is buried?'
Masters nodded.
Bullimore said: 'This I must see. Lead me to it.'
'Spades?' Masters said to Hill.
'Just one folding entrenching tool in our kit, sir.'
'That'll have to do. Come on.'

*

The bungalow was easy to find. No other stood so near to it as to allow a mistake. Masters, with only a brief pause to get his bearings, led the other five across the soft sand towards it. The top quarter inch of sand was damp. Where disturbed by their feet it uncovered the drier, paler underlayer. Beneath the green and white bungalow, the top layer was still dry, with a few pebbles, bits of coal and sticks lying about. Masters fell to his knees and peered underneath.

Bullimore said: 'It's under there?'

'Somewhere.'

Green said: 'Even if you're right, there's about six hundred square feet of ground to dig up, there. Lying down with no more than two foot of working room.'

'I hope we'll get at it fairly quickly,' said Masters. 'Here, what d'you think?' He pointed to an area just off centre. 'That part looks as if all the bits and bobs had been moved away recently, doesn't it?'

Green squatted beside him. 'Yes, I'd say so. But sheltered under here, wouldn't the marks in the sand still be there?'

Bullimore said: 'The wind whistles under these things like billyho. It gets enclosed in there and surges about strong enough to wipe out marks in no time.'

'Comforting words, Super. Now, who's going to dig?' Garner took a half step forward. Masters said: 'Thanks for the offer, but not the old and bold. It's too much to ask you to cramp up under there after flu. Hill!'

Sergeant Hill took off his coat and jacket. Brant, grinning at his companion's rueful face, undid the webbing cover of the entrenching tool. He took out the head, one half a pointed shovel, the other a pick blade. 'Pick or shovel?'

'Shovel.'

Brant slipped the short, eighteen-inch handle into the slot for converting the implement into a pixie shovel. Hill lay flat on his face and wriggled, between the bobbins, towards the spot indicated by Masters. Brant handed him the entrenching tool. Masters said: 'The graves were fairly shallow out in the open. I should think this one'll be shallower still.'

Hill, his face close to the sand said: 'Shall I probe?'

Green said: 'There's not enough height. Try and sweep the top sand away with the side of the shovel to give you a bit more depth, and we'll get you a short stick.'

Hill did as he was told, making semi-circular sweeps across his front. It was tiring work, but he refused a relief before Garner brought the stick. With this he prodded, holding the stick halfway up its length in both hands, and dragging it downwards into the sand. Despite the wind and his scanty clothing the sweat poured off his forehead as he laboured. In. Out. Move on. In. Out.

About five minutes later, the stick half buried, he looked round at Masters, without a word. Masters said quietly: 'An obstruction?'

Hill pursed his mouth in assent.

'Try a foot away in all directions.'

Masters watched him carefully. On each occasion the probe was held just below the surface. 'Good enough. Out you come.'

Hill scrambled out and dusted his front. Green gave him a cigarette and Brant handed him his clothes. Masters said: 'Right. I'm going in. It's going to be unpleasant, so have handkerchiefs ready for your noses. But while I'm in there, try to dig a trench towards me from the eastern end. We should be able to pull her out along it, head first.'

It was a tight squeeze for his great bulk, but Masters made it. With his shirt sleeves rolled up and wearing gloves, he set to work, slowly and carefully, piling up each shovel of spoil as far away as he could reach on either side. He took twenty minutes to uncover the outline of the body, and was still working away steadily, eyes down, when Brant spoke a yard or so away from his head. Brant said: 'We're trenching towards you. The Super nipped off to the Golf House and got a couple of big shovels and a rope. If we can tie it round her, we ought to be able to pull her out.'

It was a task Masters was never likely to forget. He insisted that the rope should pass under the body and round under the armpits. Brant scooped away at the sand at the upper end until he could raise the corpse slightly. Then lying so close to it that the stink of death penetrated his whole being, Masters passed his arm below her shoulders till the rope's end came out the other side. Even when the loop had been tied he refused to allow them to take the strain until the lower limbs were so far uncovered that the clinging sand would offer no resistance. Then, and only then, did he allow them to pull slowly, with himself following to guide the pitiful remains as reverently as possible along the dug pathway.

Green said, when she was clear: 'I was pleased you put it round her chest. But I couldn't have done it myself.' Masters knew what Green was thinking: what he himself had feared—that if too much strain had been placed on the rotting corpse, it might have started to disintegrate.

Bullimore said: 'I've laid on a shower for you at the Golf House.'

Masters, holding his hands and arms away from his sides, thanked him, and said to Hill: 'Give me a lift to the Golf House and then fetch me another suit from the pub. And don't forget to leave me the pHisoHex.'

Green said: 'Don't forget to ring Swaine and an ambulance.'

Chapter Five

It was twelve o'clock, and after the unpleasant activities of the morning they had all gathered in the Sundowner. Garner, Bullimore and Swaine were there.

Swaine, a strong ale in hand, said to Masters: 'I looks towards yer and raises me glass.'

Bullimore said: 'I still don't know how he did it.'

'Don't be a silly old . . . copper,' Swaine said. 'How the devil can one fathom the thought processes of a mastermind. And note the word-play.'

'It would take too long to explain. It took me half the night to arrive at the answer myself.'

'Like Einstein and his theory. He just thought for years. Then one day he ups and writes down a cryptic bit of hokum which—so I'm told—is so simple, if you're in that particular class, that it defies explanation.'

Garner, so far standing quiet among so many of his superiors, ventured a remark to Masters: 'When we were pounding the clits yesterday, I didn't think it'd come to this today.' Masters smiled, partly because he was feeling pleased with himself, partly to put Garner at his ease

Bullimore turned towards them. 'The family. They should be told. But they live in Hawksfleet.'

Masters said: 'I'm going to see them this afternoon. Would you like to warn Hawksfleet she's been found? And say that if they prefer it, I'll tell the husband.'

"You don't duck the unpleasant bits, do you?'

Masters grinned. 'I reap a lot of good from it. If I do the bad bits myself, none of my people can call me selfish when I accept the best chair available, or the best bedroom in a pub. You know the sort of thing?'

'You're too cunning for the likes of us yokels up here.' Swaine put down his glass, and to Masters' surprise, said: 'Well, I can't stay here drinking all day. There's work to be done. Grisly work. I'll probably see you tonight, Chief Inspector.'

*

After lunch the car dropped Green and Brant at 'Thrums' for the second afternoon running. Masters and Hill went on, with Garner, to Hawksfleet.

It was Julia Osborn who opened the door to Green. She said: 'You must be police officers. The two who came yesterday?'

Green said he had come specifically to speak to her. She invited them into the same room as the day before. She said: 'Dad and Berry went off to play golf.'

'In this weather?'

'In the hope of missing you, I suspect.'

Green decided he liked her. She was very reminiscent of her brother. Ginger hair and a wide, pale face and a body that needed to lose a bit of weight before it would have great appeal. Her legs were too chubby to have much form, but she had an air of youth and vitality about her and a twinkle in her eye which had been entirely lacking in the males of the family.

'Have some Turkish delight. It's gooey and powdery and fat making, but I like it so I eat it.'

Green declined, but she pressed him to have one of her father's cigars. He accepted reluctantly because of her insistence. Brant settled for a chunk of sweet, held out to him on a little plastic fork and popped into his open mouth by the girl. She said: 'It's ghastly without Mum. Nobody can come to the house because Dad says "it isn't done" under the circumstances, though he goes out womanizing every night. Berry's as pompous as a colonel from Rumblebellypore and is trying to make three of my friends all at the same time. And I'm left at home here to hold the fort. That's why I wasn't here yesterday. I stayed out late on purpose. Berry was furious because I wasn't home before dark and Dad was cross because he didn't get supper early enough to allow him to meet his bit of crumpet at the time he'd arranged.'

Green thought she'd run on for ever if he didn't stop her. 'All we came for, Miss Osborn . . .'

'Steady on there. Julia, please. I'm only eighteen, you know. Not a maiden aunt.'

'Sorry. All we want from you is a list of names of your mother's contacts. As many as you can give us.'

'I've done it. Berry told me what you wanted and that you'd suggested rummaging through old photographs to help us remember. Those poor idiots didn't even know where all the old physogs were. I raked them out this morning and had a good old . . . I nearly said laugh, when actually I wanted to cry.' She perked up again suddenly. 'But I got you scads of names, because Mummy used to write the names on the back in the old days, and I just copied them out. About a hundred and forty.'

'That's marvellous. Well, we needn't keep you, Julia, if you'll let us have the list,' said Green.

She got up, turned her back towards them and bent over to feel under the cushion of the settee. Brant looked at her. Her dress, at the back, was wrinkled up from sitting. He looked across at Green, who had his eyes fixed on the view, appreciating it. She was wearing pink, wide-legged French panties, edged with coffee-coloured lace, over a pair of tights. She turned suddenly, with the list in her hand. She said: 'Hope I didn't embarrass you, but the damn thing had slipped down the back and I had to reach over. There you are.' She gave him a couple of sheets of paper covered on both sides in round, podgy writing. He accepted it with a grin of thanks.

The car was already waiting for them as she showed them out, after pressing them unsuccessfully to stay for tea. The house which Barbara Severn had shared with her husband, Steven, and three children, was in the Hawksfleet Park. A road, bordered on the outside by good-looking houses, ran round the central grass. Masters guessed that so pleasant a view cost money, and the inside of the house seemed to indicate that Steven Severn had money to spend.

The house was double-fronted and square, of mellow red brick so cleverly used that the pointing of the courses didn't have the effect of suggesting prison walls which Masters seemed to think an inescapable feature of modern brickwork.

The door was opened by Steven Severn himself. 'You must be Chief Inspector Masters. I've been expecting you or one of your colleagues ever since I learned you had taken over the case.' Severn was a man of medium height. Square jawed and powerful. He wore grey flannels, a shirt with plain green tie and a green Braemar cardigan. His brown hair was still profuse and wavy, and his eyes were of the 'no nonsense' school.

Masters introduced Hill. They were shown into what Severn called the studio room. It was large enough to hold a private dance in. The bow window at one end was to the left of the front door. The french window at the other gave on to the lawn at the back of the house. In the middle of the side wall opposite the room door was a stained glass window—to prevent the occupants of the neighbouring property from 'looking in'—and below it a dais on which stood a baby Bechstein. Two fireplaces—one on each side of the dais—gave a deserved air of opulence, particularly because each held a blazing fire. The furniture was gracefully mixed in style and period. A gilt-legged Chesterfield upholstered in cream slipper satin in one half of the room was paired with a chintz-covered family sofa in the other. A double-bowed walnut chiffonier paired a brass-galleried table with cabriole legs. Masters liked what he saw. Felt slightly envious. Severn said: 'What can I get you?'

They declined refreshment. Masters said: 'Mr Severn, I've got a melancholy duty this afternoon.'

Severn looked straight at him. 'I've accepted that Barbara is dead. It's a logical conclusion.'

'I'm pleased you take it like that. We found Mrs Severn's body this morning.'

Severn said nothing for a moment. Then, quietly: 'She was with the others?'

Masters nodded.

'Whereabouts?'

'Under a bungalow.'

'My God, not . . .'

'Not what, Mr Severn?'

'I have a bungalow, there.'

'It wasn't your bungalow. I've looked into this, as you would expect. All the families concerned had bungalows there. Not one of them is directly implicated.'

'Maybe not, but one of my keys is missing.'

'How do you mean, missing?'

'Barbara had one on her key-ring. And that, of course, we haven't seen since Barbara disappeared.'

'I'll note that, Mr Severn. Now, can we talk, or would you rather I left you now and came back at another time?'

'Let's get it over. Please sit down. I'm forgetting the common courtesies.'

'Understandable in the circumstances.'

'Perhaps.' They sat.

Masters said: 'Please tell me what happened on the evening of the fifteenth. It was a Wednesday, I think.'

'Quite right. Barbara said she was going out to sing at the Darby and Joan party.'

'I'll have to interrupt you there, Mr Severn. "Said" she was going to sing?'

'Yes. But I found out she wasn't due there.'

'Can you explain?'

'One of Barbara's hobbies was singing. She performed quite well in her amateur way, and she sang at all sorts of gatherings and parties. Little ballads—"The Bells of Saint Mary's" and that sort of stuff. She was out and about doing it two or three times a week.'

'So it was no surprise to you when she said she was due to sing that evening?'

'No. She often sang for the Darby and Joan club. Usually in the afternoons, but this was to be the annual party, so it was to run from teatime to about nine o'clock, I think. The meetings are held in a large hut, just across the park. You can't see it from the window, but if you follow the road round or cut across the grass you'll come to it. I believe it belongs to the Ladies' Bowling Club and they let the old people have it. Anyhow, Barbara went off straight after an early dinner—before eight o'clock—and I thought no more of it until she hadn't turned up by eleven. I rang the woman who's the president or organizer of the club and asked if she knew when Barbara had set out for home, and she told me Barbara hadn't been expected there to sing at all that night, and as far as she knew, hadn't been to the hut at all.'

'I see. Can you remember when Mrs Severn first told you that she had this engagement?'

'Not exactly. A day or so beforehand, I think.'

'Was that about the usual warning you received?'

'About that. I tried to let Barbara know well in advance when I'd engagements involving both of us, but it didn't matter much if our individual engagements clashed because we have a very efficient *au pair*.'

'And your wife went out alone?'

'She had her own Mini, but as she was only going across the park she said she wouldn't take it. In fact, I can remember offering either to run her there in my car or to walk across with her, but she wouldn't let me.'

'That's understandable if she wasn't going where she said she was. Your presence might have ruined whatever plans she had. Was she happy those last few days?'

'As happy as she ever was.'

'What does that mean?'

'For a long time now I've known that Barbara felt marriage, home and family to be inadequate. She was, I think, a born do-gooder. I don't mean that in the derogatory sense. But at forty, Barbara helped with more causes and served on more committees than any other ten women. At sixty she would have been national chairman of this and that and president of the other. But even so, I never felt she got real satisfaction from it. That's why she accumulated these jobs: piled them up to keep herself busy. I've often thought it was my fault.'

'Why?'

'For marrying her. I understand you're not a married man, Chief Inspector, but you'll probably realize how it is. My God, I wanted Barbara at twenty. Not just sex, you understand, though I must admit that she was so clean limbed and . . . and desirable that I couldn't ever see myself living without her. I put every pressure on her I knew to marry me.'

'Are you saying she didn't marry you willingly?'

'Oh, she did. Apparently. But I've since thought her willingness was superficial. It was the thing to do. Get married—among your own set. You know how it is. But Barbara should have been a sort of super social worker. One of those great women who grow old helping others in out-of-the-way places of the world.'

'Instead she got a comfortable home, a fairly wealthy husband and three children.'

'Right. And they weren't enough, or they were the wrong things.'

'You're a solicitor, I believe, Mr Severn?'

'Senior partner.'

'Of a flourishing firm?'

'Very flourishing.'

Masters took out his pipe. 'Is it your considered opinion that your wife went out of her own free will to a pre-arranged meeting?'

Severn nodded. 'It wasn't a bit like Barbara really. I was certain she was as open about her affairs . . .'

'Everyday ones?'

'Oh, yes. I didn't mean affairs of the heart, because I'm as sure as a husband can be that she never had any.'

'And she wasn't being blackmailed—mentally or otherwise?'

'Certainly not otherwise. Her money and expenditure generally show no unaccounted-for amounts paid out. But mentally? Well, I suppose she could have been blackmailed mentally by anybody. I told you. Her overlarge social conscience.'

'Thank you, sir. Now I think all I want from you is a list of Mrs Severn's contacts from as far back as you can remember—from before your marriage if possible. Maybe the children can help to compile it.'

'My two eldest are away at school. The one that's here is only ten.'

'In that case, perhaps old photographs will help you recall some of the people your wife knew in the past.'

'I can do that for you straight away.'

'Could we call back for the list a bit later? In, say, an hour or an hour and a half?'

*

Green and Brant were driven, in their turn, to Hawksfleet to visit Henry Pogson. The door was opened by a small boy, whom Green thought would be seven or eight. An engaging small boy, with black hair and blue eyes and the air of a rogue. He was in brown corduroy slim fitting slacks and a fawn roll-neck sweater. He said, in a surprisingly deep voice: 'Good afternoon. I'm Tom. Who're you?'

'A policeman.'

'Are you going to bring my Mummy back?'

'Sorry, Tom, I can't. I wish I could. But I'd like to talk to Daddy if he's in.'

'He's in. He just sits in there.' Tom pointed at a door down the hallway. 'He doesn't play any more and my engine won't go.'

'I'm sorry to hear that, Tom. Will it be a big job to repair it?'

'I think it needs new . . . new . . .'

'New carbon brushes?' Brant said.

'That's right. I've only got silly sisters who can't mend engines.'

'Have you got any new brushes?'

'Yes. In a little bag.'

'Would you like me to put them in for you?'

'Yes, please.'

Green said: 'Right, Tom, can we come in? I'd like to talk to your father, and Sergeant Brant will do what he can for your engine before we go.'

'Come in. I'll tell Daddy.'

Tom walked away, leaving them to close the door. They followed him. They heard him say: 'Here's two big policemen. They want to talk to you.'

Henry Pogson came to the room door. His son had suggested he was bowled over with grief. His face and bearing seemed to underline this. A big man, formerly full faced—one would have thought—but with the flesh now hanging limply, a poor colour. The dark hair going grey. Green wondered how dark it had still been six weeks ago. The bagginess of the suit he wore indicated a sudden and great loss in weight. The eyes, however, still held some appearance of life. He said: 'Forgive me, gentlemen. I must have been dreaming. I didn't hear the door.'

'That's all right, sir. Tom did the honours,' Green said.

'The sergeant is going to mend my engine,' said Tom.

'You mustn't bother the sergeant, Tom.'

Tom said reproachfully: 'Well *you* wouldn't when I asked you.'

'Run along, Tom, and find Liz.'

The room was a comfortable study, with a desk in the bow window overlooking the garden. Three odd armchairs and a bookcase completed the furnishings, except for photographs of cricket teams around the walls, a packed cricket bag in one corner and a bat standing in a wide tin of oil. The fire was an open one, blazing well. Pogson said: 'Please sit down, gentlemen.'

'I think I'd better tell you who we are. I'm Detective Inspector Green of Scotland Yard, and this is Detective Sergeant Brant.'

'Good heavens. Have they brought the Yard in?'

Green thought it was a fair indication of Pogson's state of mind. He, one of the most concerned, was probably the only grown male in Hawksfleet and Finstoft who hadn't either read or heard that Masters and his team were there.

Green conducted the interview gently, along the same lines as before. Brenda Pogson had gone out on Sunday the nineteenth of January to play bridge. She was a bridge fan and played on an average two nights a week. This time she had left home at half past seven to join a bridge four at a house in the road parallel to the one in which she lived. She would have a walk of something more than a quarter of a mile to get there.

'Didn't the people she was supposed to play with ring up to say she hadn't arrived?' said Green.

'No. There was a fifth one there. Some old dear's sister had arrived, and she'd taken her along, so they didn't really worry about Brenda.'

'You mean nobody even thought to inquire?'

'They started without her. Then they got immersed in the game. If you knew these bridge fiends you'd realize that once the fever's on them everything but the game is driven from their minds, and nothing on earth would prise them loose from the table.' He sounded bitter. Green guessed he was blaming the bridge four for not phoning. Probably, Pogson thought, that had they reacted to her non-appearance, something might have been done to save her. Though what could have been done, Green couldn't imagine.

'You're sure your wife intended to go to the bridge party?' said Green.

'She said so, and they were expecting her.'

'Did the woman whose sister arrived ring your wife, by any chance?'

'Miss Ingoldby? Yes, she did. That afternoon. Brenda took the call in here and I can remember her saying she was sure the Slades wouldn't mind the sister going along.'

'Thank you. Now, Mr Pogson, what time did you expect your wife back?'

'About eleven. Not earlier. They'd play till their eyes popped out.'

'And it was only after that that you began to get worried?'

'I rang the Slades at half past eleven. Brenda had then been gone four hours. I phoned the police immediately, put my eldest daughter—she's fifteen—to phone everybody we knew to find out if they'd seen Brenda, and then set off myself, on foot, to look for her.'

Green thought that Pogson must have idolized his wife. He certainly wasn't the one to worry about impressions where her safety was concerned. He said to Pogson: 'You were baby-sitting?'

'In a way. I was combining that duty with pleasure.'

'Oh?'

'I'm a member of the cricket club . . .'

'So I gathered.'

'I'm also an accountant, so it's almost inevitable that I should be appointed treasurer.'

Green nodded.

'Our A.G.M. was fixed for Tuesday the twenty-first, and I had to present the accounts. The club does an internal audit, you know. I'd arranged to have that done on the Sunday night, here. Our secretary, Harry Burn and another committee member, George White, were the board. They came round here—just before Brenda set out, actually—and were here until after ten. The accounts didn't take more than an hour, but we sat down over a drink to have a chat.'

'Replaying old matches?'

For the first time there was a slight smile from Pogson. 'Yes. I suppose we're every bit as bad as the bridge players in that respect.'

'Just one more question, sir. Did your wife get another telephone call that Sunday afternoon?'

Pogson didn't have to think. 'Yes. But who from, I don't know. You see, Inspector, I've been over all this again and again in my mind. Searching for some reason, some clue. But I missed that call. I was playing trains with Tom by then—up in his bedroom. I heard the phone and knew Brenda answered it. It was obviously a private one for her, because she didn't call me, and the kids say nobody rang them that afternoon. But naturally I didn't ask Brenda, and in any case I'd forgotten about it when she called us down to tea. Now I'm left wondering whether that call could have had any bearing on her disappearance; and I suspect you are, too.'

'We like to consider all possibilities, sir.' Green didn't expand his statement. He went on to ask for a list of Mrs Pogson's contacts, and while it was being prepared, Brant went off to find Tom and renew the carbon brushes.

*

Christopher Baker himself admitted Masters and Hill. He was a pleasant man. Fair haired, brown eyed, with healthily tanned skin and a fair moustache. He gave an impression of being well washed. His leisure clothes were old, but obviously of good quality and well cared for. He was nearly as tall as Masters, but much slimmer built. There was the air of an athlete about him. He smoked a pipe with a curly stem. It was in his hand as he greeted them at the door of the detached villa in Roche Close.

He said, cheerfully: 'Come in and join the family. We're home-birds, these days, but the kids are beginning to champ at the bit. Now you've come they're hoping this business will be cleared up and we'll be able to get back to normal as far as possible without Cynthia.'

'Your children are taking their mother's disappearance well?' asked Masters.

'Better than I could have hoped. They're twenty and nineteen, you know, so I suppose I ought to have known.'

'And you?'

'Me? I'm doing my best—for them. Every so often it gets a bit much, but Cyn and I—and the kids for that matter—didn't wear our hearts on our sleeves. We understood one another, you see, so we could pretend to be a bit blasé. It's best in the long run, otherwise we'd be moping now. Instead, d'you know what we're doing? Playing three-handed Ludo and waiting for Sara's boy friend to come along to make a fourth.' He ushered them across the hall and into the sitting-room. The Ludo board was on a stool in front of the fire. 'Meet Sara and Royce.'

Sara Baker, at twenty, was a girl who at a first meeting struck one as knowing that she looked good without much effort on her part. It had all been done for her at birth. She was ash blonde with a beautiful face and eyes put in with sooty fingers. She wore a simple black frock. The unembroidered purity of its line must have exercised a master in the art, and had he seen Sara in it, he would have wept at the perfection he had created. Her voice had just a trace of huskiness—a drawl that might—if disembodied—have sounded supercilious, but which, backed by her smile and gay eyes was devastatingly attractive. Masters could tell that her father, as he introduced her, worshipped her. His son, Royce, was a fine specimen, too. Nearly six feet tall, nearly as fair as his sister, with hair that waved, god-like, above his ears. His nose was straight, his eyes humorous, and his handshake firm. Unlike his sister, he was dressed casually, in almost white slacks and a fair-isle patterned sloppy joe.

Baker said in reply to Masters' question: 'We're civil engineers specializing in land reclamation, though we'll build you anything you like, won't we, Royce? Strictly between ourselves, Mr Masters, Royce has ideas about bridges, but nobody seems to be buying many these days. Still, he's learning fast.'

'Land reclamation?'

'There's a host of it to be done within striking distance of here. From the Yorkshire coast, down through the fens to the Wash. These are our main stamping grounds.'

Sara said: 'I'll ask Clarice to bring some tea. She's our very present helpmeet, Mr Masters, and one of your fans. She told me in the kitchen this morning that now you're on the job it won't be long before it's cleared up.'

'I hope I justify her trust in me.' Masters turned to Baker. 'Now, sir? What happened here on the evening of . . . when was it? Saturday the twenty-fifth?'

'I honestly don't know. I was out. I'd been to have a haircut in the afternoon. Latish. It was half past five when I left the chair. There was a friend of mine there—Bishop's his name—at the same time. As we left, the barber locked up behind us. Bishop said: "One door closes, another opens. The Ace of Spades is open. How about a quickie?" Nothing loath, I agreed, and we were there drinking for over an hour. It was after seven when I got home. The kids had gone off somewhere. Sara with her fiancé and Royce with a nice bit of homework I wouldn't mind myself . . .' He winked at Royce as he said it. Royce grinned. His father went on: 'Cynthia was putting on her coat and hat. She told me Clarice would give me my meal. She, Cynthia, was going off to visit a friend of hers whose daughter's getting married at Easter. Cynthia was a bit of a designer—hats and things—millinery or whatever it's called—as a hobby, you know—and she'd promised to think up some snazzy sort of headgear for the bridesmaids.'

'Was your wife's visit to her friend pre-arranged? Had she mentioned it to you earlier?'

'Not a word, otherwise I wouldn't have gone with Bishop to the Ace of Spades. And as for pre-arrangement—well, you can make what you like of it. When Cynthia didn't return, I rang up, and she'd never arrived. Said they weren't expecting her specifically that night. There was just a vague arrangement that Cynthia should drop in sometime, as and when she liked.'

Masters thanked him. Sara had returned, and close behind her Clarice, with the tea. Sara introduced Clarice to Masters. It was clear the middle-aged woman was thrilled to meet him and she asked if there was anything she could do to help bring the murderer of her mistress to book. She was delighted when Masters said that there was something she could do. Make a list—in conjunction with the family—of all Cynthia Baker's contacts.

*

It was past six o'clock when, the party complete with their lists of names, returned to the Estuary. Masters said to Garner: 'I'm not inviting you in for a drink just now.'

'Right, sir.'

'Your wife will be expecting you, won't she?'

'Yes, sir. Kippers for tea every Sunday at our house. They'll be waiting for me.'

'That's what I thought. But could you return later? Say at half past eight?'

Garner seemed only too willing to come. Masters said: 'Those lists. I want some local knowledge. My two sergeants will be collating them. I want you present, just in case. Your wife won't mind?'

'She's been a copper's wife for long enough, sir. She'll probably pop out to her sister's anyhow. She usually does, Sunday nights.'

When Garner had gone, they walked into the foyer. Tintern was standing by the reception desk, complaining to the manager. Masters overheard a little of it and halted to hear the rest. Tintern was saying: '. . . and she wouldn't allow me to use it. She refused to unlock it.'

'Because the washer had gone on one of the hot taps, sir, and we'd had to turn the water off in that bathroom, otherwise the whole hotel would have been out of hot water.'

'Because the washer had gone on one of the hot taps? Last week I couldn't use one of the lavatories.'

'I explained that too, sir. We have to do our decorating in the winter. We only put one lavatory out of action at a time. There are more than thirty in the hotel.'

'More than thirty in the hotel? I had to walk a mile to find one.'

Masters and his party moved on. Green said: 'He's always grousing. A real crabby arse.'

'Artistic temperament,' said Hill.

'Artistic? He's just plain mardy.'

'Who's for a drink?' Masters asked.

The Sundowner was empty except for Shirl. She said: 'You found the fifth 'un, then? When're you going to get the bloke who did it?'

'Give us a chance,' said Green.

'To do what?'

Green grinned: 'If we hadn't company present I'd tell you.'

At that moment Tintern came down the stairs. Masters noticed that he had changed his shirt and was very spruce and well shaven. To their surprise, he said gaily: 'Ah! There you are, Chief Inspector. I understand I have to congratulate you.'

'Thank you, Mr Tintern.'

This was the first time he had spoken to them. Yet he was treating them like old pals. 'Always knew you'd do it. Professionals, that's what you are. Come along, gentlemen, drink up. I must buy you a celebratory drink.'

'Well, Mr Tintern, we've already got pints,' said Green.

'Already got pints? Never mind. There'll be plenty of room where that's going to. Or if not, what about a gin? Foursome's gin. That's what I always have.'

'Foursome's gin? I don't think I know it. Is it London or Plymouth?' said Masters.

Tintern clapped him on the back, and said with a laugh: 'Is it London or Plymouth? There's a joke. It's Hawksfleet. Pure Hawksfleet.' He pointed to the far end of Shirl's shelves. 'There it is, look. One, two, three, four, fifth from the end, second shelf, between those two red bottles.'

Green looked at Masters and raised his eyebrows. Masters looked in the direction indicated. He could see the Foursome's gin label—two mixed pairs of golfers holing a drink in one at the nineteenth tee—but no red bottles. There were, however, coloured fairy bulbs round the shelves. Probably some trick of the light made the two flanking bottles look red to Tintern. They were plain glass to Masters.

'I've seen yellow gin . . .' began Hill.

Masters silenced him with a look.

Green said: 'I'll try anything once.' Brant simply looked bewildered.

'You'll try anything once? Good,' said Tintern. 'Then we'll need five doubles, with water for me and what? Tonic? For the rest of you? Shirl! Shirl. Ah, there you are, Shirl. Five Foursomes, doubles, and four tonics. These gentlemen need a good stiff drink after climbing about over the clits all day in this weather.' He turned to Masters just behind him—the other three had gathered in a close group and were paying no attention at the moment—'Tell me, Chief Inspector, when do you expect to get your man?'

'I really don't know, Mr Tintern.'

'You really don't know! Hear that, Shirl? The modesty of the man.'

Masters accepted his gin and raised the glass to Tintern. At the same time he wondered why the finding of the fifth body should cause the architect to buy them a drink.

Chapter Six

After dinner, while the sergeants and Garner were tabulating the lists of contacts in Hill's bedroom, Masters and Green went to the Sundowner in the hope of meeting Swaine. On the way, Masters stopped to catch the roving drinks waiter, who was serving the billiard and card rooms, to order a tray of bottled beer to be sent up to the workers. They caught him at the door to the card room. Tintern was at a bridge table. He was playing the hand but he looked up and saw them. He waved gaily and then went on, piling up the tricks at his left elbow.

Green said, as they walked across the foyer: 'Comic cuts, that chap. I suppose architecting a cathedral is artistic work. But I never think using a ruler and a compass is art. I call it geometry. Still, he must have a flair for it, even if he is a bit kinked.'

'You know, I don't believe in artistic temperament,' said Masters. 'I believe that most successful creative men have a bit of the woman about them which gives them just that little bit keener, finer mind for artistry. The only real artistic temperament in my opinion comes to light at the last moment, when performers are screwing themselves up to the right pitch for putting on a good show. I don't know about Tintern. He's a bit of a scream, I suppose. Anyhow, the staff here treat him like one.'

'They're harmless, his type. He's not one of your vicious nancy boys,' Green said.

They went down the steps to the Sundowner. Swaine was already there. 'They'll bring your drinks now they've seen you're here. Park your carcases and tell me the news.'

'None.'

Swaine laughed. 'The penalty of fame. You're expected to produce the goods at every touch and turn.'

'This case is as odd as Dick's hatband. I've got a feeling we're getting close, but I can't for the life of me put a finger on my reason for saying so,' said Masters.

Swaine said: 'Wishful thinking, old boy. Ah! Here it comes. I've got a thirst on me I wouldn't sell for a fiver on a Saturday night. I've been saving it up till you came.'

Shirl put the drinks down. She said: 'Just wave when you're ready for more if it's to be the same again.'

'It will be, my dear. It will be.' Swaine patted her rump as she turned away. The sound was a dull thud, like knocking on wood. He said: 'My God, she's got the iron curtain in there. Both sides of it.'

Shirl turned and grinned. 'None of your cheek, Doctor.'

'None of mine, old girl. You've got enough in there with your own two.'

'You've examined Barbara Severn?' Masters said.

Swaine nodded: 'Report'll be word for word like the others. Asphyxiation through manual strangulation. Nose broken. No scratches. No bruises except those expected from the strangler's hands. No change. Except this one was a bit further gone.'

Green offered Swaine a Kensitas; Masters filled his pipe. Green said: 'It doesn't make sense.'

Swaine said: 'Of course it doesn't. Nothing a madman does ever makes sense.'

'That's a point. Look here, Doctor. You said madman. What does that mean? I know in the old days it meant anybody with any one of a hundred different neuroses or derangements. They were sent to the madhouse. But what does it mean today?' Masters asked.

'You've answered your own question. Any one of a hundred different states. And I don't mean straws in the hair or a complex which leads you to think you're Napoleon.'

'What then?'

'Oh, lord. Now you've got me. I told you I was no psychiatrist. And quite honestly I don't think I can help you off hand. But if you really think it's important. . . .'

Masters said quietly: 'I think I do. I may be wrong, but I don't think I am.'

'Right. I could read up a bit, tomorrow. I've got a few books.'

'Lend them to me. I can probably satisfy myself at first hand better than you could second hand.'

'Suits me. I've got things I'd rather do than plough through worm-eaten text books on psychiatry. When d'you want them?'

'I'll collect them tonight—when you go home.'

Swaine stared a moment. 'Bedtime reading, eh? By cripes you're keen, or . . .' He paused. '. . . or you're sure of yourself. I don't know which. And I don't care. Ready for more ale?'

'My turn.' Masters put a pound note on the table to await Shirl, and then said: 'Don't run away with the idea that I'm saying we've solved the case. We haven't.'

Green said: 'You're telling the world!'

'It's a tough 'un. As tough as Billy Whitlam's bulldog. And until we get more information my nose isn't itching, so I can't tell whether I'm kissed, crossed or vexed. But Green'll tell you there comes a time when you get a feeling about a case.'

'When they start to come sweet. Finding that corpse this morning helped, though I wouldn't exactly call that sweet, myself. Still, you can't have it all ways. Finding a woman in any state is pretty bad, but it's when you find kids battered that your blood boils—or mine does, and I wouldn't say I was particularly keen on kids, where I am keen on women. Odd, that, isn't it?'

Swaine laughed. 'It's so normal as to be distinctly odd.'

Green sucked his teeth. 'I'm pleased about that. Sometimes I'm made to think that even just being a policeman shows I've got some sort of a kink.'

'No doubt. Not that being a policeman normally shows anything but a liking for the work. But some coppers, somewhere, are in their jobs solely for the feeling of power it gives them. And that's the trouble with complexes and neuroses. They often go unsuspected by the world at large because they affect only part of a person's psyche. It's only when that part increases so much as to become noticeable that people begin to look at each other and touch their temples significantly.'

'What brings it on, or causes it to increase? Has it to be there in the first place?' Masters asked.

'Dunno. Some are born with it, others have it thrust upon them, so to speak. Pressure of modern living, perhaps. Even a single experience, devastating enough, can trigger off all sorts of nasties. Mental shock. You've seen horror films. Apparently normal people turn into gibbering idiots at the sight of something outlandish. I've never known it happen quite like that. People usually progress towards a neurosis—some more quickly than others.'

'When you're ready to go, I'll come with you for those books.'

Swaine stared in surprise. 'Hold your water, old boy. There's a lot of good drinking time left. Half an hour at least.'

Masters turned to Green. 'In that case, would you mind going with the doc to pick up his books. I want a word with that lot upstairs.'

Masters was just about to leave when Bullimore arrived. In a dark, civilian suit the Superintendent looked more chunky than ever. His face was scrubbed and shone glossily red in the lights. His collar looked so tight that Masters expected him to puff at every word he spoke.

'I thought you'd be here. Now we've got Mrs Severn we can include her in the inquest tomorrow. I've seen the coroner and he wants to know if we'd like an adjournment?'

'No. If he adjourns till we've got evidence as to who the killer is, it'll mean I'll have to come up here to give it to him, simply so's he can name the name in the verdict. And I don't want that. As it is now, because you were with us this morning, you can give evidence about finding all the bodies. Tell him to cut it short. Evidence of identification, medical evidence to show cause of death, and very little else. It's so obviously murder in all five cases he won't even need to ask the families any questions other than those necessary to establish dates of death. Then he can bring in a verdict against person or persons unknown and we'll be left free to play it our way.'

'That's what I expected you'd want, but I thought I'd better check. You're not going, are you? Stay and have one with me. Go on, man, fill your boots.'

Masters sat down again, and joined in desultory conversation until Shirl called time. Bullimore offered to run him and Swaine home for the books.

Masters was given the freedom of the doctor's bookshelves. He was interested in all the volumes, but finally concentrated on one group, a series, all similarly bound. Out of these he chose seven titles: *Psychosis, Insanity, Behaviour, Disorientation, Temperament, Mind,* and *Dementia.* Put together, the slim books could be held in one hand: each a part of the whole which ran to twenty-four volumes. When he had made his choice, Swaine took them from him and gave him a strong ale in their stead. Swaine said: 'You know, I nearly slung these out about six months ago. I was conned into buying them when I had a rush of enthusiasm to the head about psychiatry a year or two back. I don't think I've read one of them. I find if I stick to Martindale I don't go very far wrong these days. However, you might find yourself getting a psychosis of your own trying to plough through this lot without a medical dictionary.' He turned to the bookcase. 'Here you are. A little one. Pocket size.'

Bullimore drove Masters back to the Estuary and dropped him at the door. Masters made his way up to Hill's room. He found Garner still there, and Green eating a packet of crisps. He said: 'Finished?'

Hill picked up a sheaf of papers from the bed. One sheet for every letter of the alphabet that occurred as the initial of a surname in the lists they had collected. Each sheet was divided into five columns, and in each column were the names of each of the dead woman's contacts in alphabetical order. Hill said: 'Two pairs. Two Mary Starkeys. Two Mrs Robert Trings.'

'Is that all?'

'Except for christian names again. They overlap in scores of places.'

Masters took the armchair and laid his books beside him on the carpet. 'Anybody got any ideas?'

Nobody replied.

'Garner?'

'Well, of course, sir, I recognize a lot of the names, but there's plenty round here I know by sight without their names.'

'Of course. Now. Mary Starkey. She was the girl who appeared twice on Frances Burton's school photograph. She was at the Finstoft girls' school, so she would also be on Joanna Osborn's list.'

Brant said: 'No. On Cynthia Baker's.'

'But Joanna Osborn is the other Finstoft woman.'

'Maybe she is now. But was she before she was married? She might be a Hawksfleet woman or, and this is another angle, though Cynthia Baker now lives in Hawksfleet, she may have lived in Finstoft as a girl.'

Masters began slowly to fill his pipe. 'Can't we tell from the lists? We know Frances Burton knew Mary Starkey. If one of the other murdered women knew Frances Burton, it's likely she'd know Starkey, too.'

'They all knew each other,' said Brant.

'Oh.'

'And it doesn't follow that the friends of friends are friends. So we're up the creek,' added Green.

Masters lit his pipe. When it was going, he said: 'We're not, you know. I've made a mistake by not warning you all to get christian names and maiden names. We've got Mary Starkey twice. And Mrs Robert Tring twice. Couldn't Mary Starkey have married and become Mrs Tring?'

'She could. But it's long odds,' said Green.

'Are you sure?'

"Course I'm not sure, but it's a shot I wouldn't care to bet on. Put it that way.'

Masters tamped his pipe and said: 'Tell me where I've gone wrong. I consider it logical to suppose that five women in the same stratum of society, of the same age, and living in the same isolated conurbation would have at least one mutual contact.'

'That's logical enough. They all knew each other. And that means you have five mutual contacts—all dead.'

'But a common factor?'

Green lit a Kensitas. 'I know what you mean, and what you want. I've no argument with that. It's routine police procedure to look for common factors in similar crimes. But you've got them. Broken noses, no scratches, similar graves. Oodles of them.'

'You're making me doubt myself,' said Masters.

'What good would a common contact do us if we found one?' Hill asked.

Masters looked across at him and said: 'Somehow these five women are linked. Right?'

'We've agreed they weren't just picked at random out of the whole female population. But couldn't they have been picked at random out of one set of women?'

Masters nodded. 'They could. And it makes no difference. Those five knew each other. If our man were to kill again, would all six have known each other?'

'Probably.'

'Then probably there's another woman in this area who is in danger simply because she knew and was known to the other five. I don't say there is, but we mustn't assume that a man who has killed five times will stop there. And if there is the slightest chance that his choice is not random, I want to know who the sixth person— presumably an acquaintance of all five previous victims—is likely to be. That's why I want us to sift and sift and sift again until we either find such a woman or we are positive no such woman exists. In fact, there may be more than one.'

'So we're out to stop this loony from operating again,' said Green.

'That, of course. But if we could run such a woman to earth, we might be able to find the link which she may not even suspect exists.'

Brant said: 'And the link presumably points to the murderer.'

'It may not point directly, but it should be a help.'

'O.K.,' said Green. 'Supposing you're right about Starkey being Tring. That's a common contact for only four.'

'Somebody's forgotten her. It was bound to happen. Who was it?'

'Pogson.'

'The nervous one. He produced the list on his own. All the others had help. I'd expect him to forget more than the others.' Masters got to his feet. 'We'll check tomorrow. Me for beddy-byes.'

*

Masters lay propped up, with Swaine's small books scattered around him. He glanced through at chapter headings, looking for he knew not what. For over an hour he read bits and pieces of information about psychiatric disorders, trying to study behavioural patterns, using his dictionary as he went. Logging the attitudes and fantasies of the insane in a so-called age of reason. He found it heavy going. Nothing to help him. Dementia praecox—he'd heard that before. An old name for general mental deficiency or madness, wasn't it? Better make sure. He picked up the dictionary and found the meaning. He read it carefully and then reached for the book on Dementia. For more than another hour he read carefully, and then lay back thinking for twenty minutes before turning out the light and settling down to sleep.

*

At breakfast the next morning Green said: 'Well, I suppose we've got to go round all these houses again. Are we going to the same places we went to before?'

Masters had ordered scrambled eggs, fried bacon and mushrooms. He had his mouth full when Green spoke, so there was no answer for a moment. Then: 'I'd like you to do the lot. If you're in luck there should be only three places to visit.'

'And you?'

'I don't quite know where I shall go. I've several places in mind.'

Hill and Brant exchanged glances. Green said: 'I could do with a day off, too.'

'You'll be glad you didn't take the day off if you see Sara Baker. I wouldn't mind visiting her on a Monday morning myself,' Hill said.

'Your trouble is you're sex-orientated, lover-lugs,' Green said.

'Thank God.'

Masters called for more toast. 'Anybody seen Tintern this morning?'

Deadly Pattern

Brant told him that Tintern had had fruit juice and toast earlier, and had now left. Green said: 'What d'you want him for?'

'I wondered if he'd give me a conducted tour of his church. It's one of the places I'd like to visit. I'm interested in old buildings.'

Green took Masters's last piece of toast and spread it savagely with butter and marmalade.

*

Masters and Hill waited for Garner. Green and Brant took the car. Masters said to Garner: 'I want to visit a gymnasium—boxing, wrestling. That sort of place.'

'Feeling like a work-out, chief? If so, choose somebody your own size,' said Hill.

Masters didn't reply. He stood with his hands in his coat pockets, back to the wind, waiting for Garner's mind to turn over.

'You know, sir, I don't think there is one.'

'No trainer with a makeshift ring in a shed?'

'There may be one in Hawksfleet, but I'll have to check up to find out.'

'Slip along then. Use the phone inside the foyer. Tell them to charge it to me.'

Garner went inside. Masters and Hill crossed the road and stood looking at the gardens, where two council workmen had started to straighten up after the gales of the last week. The sun came out, pale and weak. The tide, ebbing, looked greasily flat and dirty. Masters said nothing. He just stood. Hill guessed he preferred not to be disturbed.

Garner came out. 'I rang the Hawksfleet duty sergeant. He says there are two, both backstreet mills.'

'Can you take us there?'

'On a bus, sir. There'll be a bit of a walk at the far end, though.'

They recrossed the road and waited at the bus stop. The journey took them past the Prawner where they'd lunched on the first day, and along the main road connecting the two towns. There was no gap, no demarcation line to show the boundary, but where, on the Finstoft section of the road there had been mainly houses, with a few shops, in Hawksfleet there were mainly shops and dingy business premises: a dentist's sign, a Methodist chapel, a woodyard, garages and empty premises, grimy beyond measure, garnished with auctioneers' boards screaming out the vacant square footage or telling blatant lies about the desirability of the property.

As if apologizing, Garner said: 'This is the road to the docks. It's not the best part of the town.'

From his seat on the top deck, Masters surveyed the scene, unaware of its drabness, of the gossiping women, young and old, but all alike in wearing garish bedroom slippers and dingy headscarves from below which peeped metal hair curlers. He was thinking hard. What was it Swaine had said? One single devastating experience? What had the medical dictionary said? A large group of psychoses of psychogenic origin, often recognized during or shortly after adolescence but frequently in later maturity? He'd learned it off by heart. Could he combine the two? If so . . .

Garner said: 'Next stop, sir.'

Masters got up and led the way downstairs. After a wait for a lull in the traffic they crossed another main road coming in at right angles. Just before a level crossing, Garner turned off left, down a narrow passage. Monday, washday. Already lines in the little back gardens on either side were heavy with grey-looking clothes and linen that would have delighted an ad-man's heart if he were looking out for 'before' shots to advertise washing powders. There was no brightness and whiteness in this laundry.

Garner turned into a small street, block-ended by sleepers guarding the railway lines. He crossed and entered another passage. The scream of a circular saw seared the brain. The dull thud and chink of shunting numbed the senses. At last, side on, between the passage and the railway, a two-storied wooden shed, leaning slightly, but stoutly built and tarred on the outside to keep it weatherproof. The double door at ground level was padlocked. An outside flight of steps made of treads with no risers led up to a door with a flaking notice: 'Cyril Cass. Office.'

They went up. Without knocking, Garner entered. In the green-painted lobby a kettle stood on a gas ring and half a dozen dirty mugs, a milk bottle and an open bag of sugar sat on a beer advertisement tin tray. Faded pictures of boxers, all of whom faced the camera fiercely, lined the walls.

Three doors led off the lobby. Masters knocked on the one marked 'Private' and entered. 'Mr Cass?'

He was a little man. Bald. Pink faced. He looked as if he'd been born in the roll neck sweater made of fisherman's abb with the natural oil still in it. 'Yes. Who're you?'

'I'm a police officer.'

'Are yer? And a big 'un, too. Dreadnought class I shouldn't wonder, which 'ud make it tricky to match yer. Whatcher want?'

'A little help, I hope.'

'Thass a change. Although I'll say this, I ain't had much trouble from your mob. Help?'

The office was brown varnish all over, like the inside of a chapel cloakroom. The air was compounded of rancid emulsion, sweat, smoke, and coke fumes. The tortoise stove in the corner was glowing red at the top. The windows appeared to be nailed up and blacked out with grime.

'Help?'

'Yes, Mr Cass. Can we all come in?'

'Well, count me out! You've brought your seconds wi' yer, I see.'

Masters sat on a high square stool with a leathercloth top polished black by generations of backsides. 'Mr Cass, if you wanted to knock somebody out, what would you do?'

'Uppercut to the point.'

'Would that leave a bruise?'

'As like as not.'

'If you were wearing ordinary civilian gloves. Not four ouncers.'

'Then it would for sure. Nasty bruise.'

'Right. But what if you didn't want to leave a bruise?'

Cass considered this for a moment. He put his feet up on his cluttered desk. He was wearing thick-soled, blue deck shoes. Then: 'Can't be done.'

'It can. It has.'

'Not under Queensberry rules.'

'Maybe not. But consider foul play.'

Cass thought again. 'You've come to the wrong place, mister. You want Shen.'

'What's that?'

'It's a he. Judo boy—black belt or summat he calls hisself. Over in Acre Yard.'

'Judo? Thanks. I thought it might be that.' Masters turned to Garner. 'Know Acre Yard?'

'Never heard of it, sir.'

Cass directed them.

Shen Ma Pang was courteous, but wary. Unlike the Cass office, his gymnasium was clean. Spotless, but small. There was a heap of sponge rubber fall mats in one corner. But the bare floor shone. Shen was in a navy blue suit and cream shirt. It was difficult to tell his age, because he was so sparely built, but Masters thought he must be at least sixty.

When he had been ushered in, Masters explained who he was. Shen bowed in assent when asked for help. Masters said: 'I want you to tell me if it is possible to make an opponent unconscious without leaving a bruise.'

Shen looked at him very steadily.

'You have seen this done?'

'Not witnessed it being carried out.'

'But it has happened?'

Masters nodded.

'It is a hold nobody should use,' said Shen.

'But it can be done?'

Shen nodded. 'But not when opponent wears correct clothing.'

'You mean the blouse and loose trousers the wrestlers wear?'

'That is what I mean.'

'Mr Shen, do you teach judo?'

'For forty years I teach ju-jitsu. During war I teach under secrets in Hampshire.'

'So that if somebody round here were to use this particular hold he would most likely be a pupil of yours?'

Shen bowed.

Masters said: 'You teach this hold to all your pupils?'

'No. It is for black belt only.'

'Could you tell me what the hold is?'

'For attacker wearing coat. I show you.'

Shen approached Hill, who manfully stood his ground. Shen said: 'Please, do not struggle.' The next moment, Hill was being lowered to the ground unconscious. Shen said: 'Please do not worry. He will be all right soon.'

Though it seemed like minutes to Masters, Hill was out for less than thirty seconds. He sat up, none the worse, but unaware of exactly what had happened to him. As soon as Masters was satisfied that he had suffered no harm, he turned to Shen who said: 'No bruises.'

'Where?'

'Anywhere.'

'I didn't see exactly what you did. Would you demonstrate slowly, please.'

Shen shook his head. 'It is forbidden.'

'I think you may have shown this hold to somebody in the past.'

'Not shown.'

Masters ignored the denial. 'And the person to whom you demonstrated it has killed five women.'

Shen held up his hands, palm foremost. 'He would not kill without bruising.'

'Let's stop arguing, my friend. I have a killer to catch. Please show me the hold.'

'Very well.'

Shen again stepped up to Hill who took a step back. 'I will not make you unconscious this time.' Hill stood. Shen went through the motions slowly. First he crossed his hands at the wrist. He then reached up until he could grasp Hill's coat collar on either side of the neck below the ears. 'This is the grip. The only strength needed is in the fingers to maintain the grip. It is the wrist bone of each hand which flicks the nerve on each side of the neck. It has to be known where the nerve is. A jerk of the wrist jars the nerves and brings unconsciousness but leaves no bruises. Long, hard pressure brings death and leaves bruises.' Shen dropped his arms. Masters examined Hill's neck. There was no sign of a bruise: possibly a slight redness, but Masters could not even be sure of that.

Shen refused further information. He would not point out the exact run of the nerves, pleading that to show this hold was dangerous and forbidden. Masters was satisfied. He asked to see the lists of Shen's pupils for years back. He spent forty minutes going through the lists, while Shen made pale tea for them. As they left he said to Shen: 'You never teach that hold, you say?'

'Never to Englishmen.'

'Then how . . .?'

'Some people may get more than cold in the eye from peeping through keyholes.'

'I see. Thank you.'

On the way back, Hill said: 'Well, now we know how it was done, but do we know who?'

Masters refused to be drawn. He merely said: 'Back to the Estuary.'

He was still preoccupied. They were on the bus bound for home when he said: 'Is there a registrar in Finstoft?'

Garner replied: 'If we get off a few stops before the Estuary, we can cut through the old bit of the town. He's not got a proper office. What I mean is, he works from his own front room.'

'Does he keep his records there?'

Garner scratched his head. 'Now you've got me, sir. But I don't think he can do. It's a bare old room he's got. Just a table and a typewriter and a hell of a lot of dust. I shouldn't think his missus has been in to clean him up these last twenty years.'

'Probably she's not paid to.'

'That's about the size of it. D'you want to see him?'

'Yes.'

Hill stayed out of the conversation. He knew the signs when Masters went broody. Interruptions to his thoughts at such times sent the chief up the wall. Hill wondered whether piecing the final bits of a case together worried Masters. It seemed to. Hill thought that if he, himself, could sew up cases as well as Masters, he would be elated every time he did it. He thought that Green, in the same place, would carry a flag.

'This is it,' said Garner, and led the way downstairs. Masters understood why this would be the old part of Finstoft. It was higher than the rest. The place that would be chosen because it was above the flood-water level. They cut inland from the sea front. Dropping down a narrow street flanked with shops. The sort of shops Masters liked. The family butcher, the old established greengrocer, the cluttered newspaper shop, a real tobacconist's with brown varnished front and fascia board carved with the owner's name. A pub that looked like a pub, not a supermarket. A grocer who roasted his own coffee, with the smell coming out of a wide pipe above the shop doorway. He appreciated them all, subconsciously. Even the barber's shop, which had a proper pole and a display of old-fashioned, twin-funnelled shaving mugs.

The pavements were narrow and flagged with uneven stone, not concrete slabs. The kerbs were worn shallow, and the traffic had difficulty in edging its way past the parked lorries discharging their wares into the shops. They walked in single file, rounding other pedestrians and avoiding push chairs. Then they were clear of the bottleneck. Garner turned left at the cross roads, passed the Salvation Army Hall and an interesting smelling ironmonger's, and halted opposite a terrace of Victorian houses with wooden bays and small asphalted front gardens. The door plate announced that Charles Summerhead, Registrar for births, deaths and marriages was present for business between nine and one, and two and five every day except Saturday, when one o'clock was his finishing time.

Deadly Pattern

They crossed the road. Garner led the way in. He said: 'Morning, Charlie, this here's Detective Chief Inspector Masters of Scotland Yard. He wants to talk to you.'

The room was as bare as Garner had said it would be. A gas-fire sputtered on the uncurbed hearth of cracked, grass-green tiles. Behind it the old period-piece cast iron fireplace still stood to harbour dirt and top-off the air of dejection in the room. Summerhead was very bald, with a soft, pinkish face that reminded Masters of a carnival mask. He wore gold-rimmed spectacles and a stiff, round-cornered collar. His suit was shiny blue. Masters thought that Summerhead must have stopped being a human being the moment he became a registrar, but had continued to live like a performing cabbage capable of filling in four or five different proformas only because the information given on each was roughly the same, but put down in a different order.

Summerhead looked over his spectacles at Masters. 'And what can I do for you?' It was querulous: hopeful that he wouldn't be asked to do too much.

'Save me a trip to Somerset House.'

'It will cost you a search fee.'

'Will it? Send the bill into the local Superintendent.'

'Cash. One and ninepence. *If* I help you. What d'you want to know?'

Masters turned to Hill and Garner. 'We passed a good tobacconist's just now. That sort of place will stock Warlock Flake. Get me two ounces.'

Having got rid of the other two, Masters said: 'I'd like to see your register of births for forty to forty-five years back, please.'

Summerhead grumbled, but obviously thought it better to humour Masters. A metal cupboard was opened and the relevant volumes found. Two books, wider than they were long, covered the period. Summerhead said: 'Who is it you want to know about?'

'D'you mind if I look myself? There can't be so many births each year in Finstoft.'

'Best part of five hundred,' said Summerhead, bridling as if Masters had accused him of having no work to do; no happy events to record.

Masters knew what he was looking for. He sped through. Even so it took him nearly twenty-five minutes to find what he wanted. A brief glance was all he needed, but to put off the watchful Summerhead he continued thumbing through for another five minutes. Then he paid his one and ninepence and left. Hill and Garner were waiting outside. Hill handed him his tin of tobacco and the change. Garner led them back to the Estuary.

*

The two of them were in Masters's room. Green said: 'I've had one hell of a time getting it. All those men were at work.'

'So?'

'Julia Osborn told me. Starkey is Tring.'

'Good. That's what I like to hear. Did you get hold of Pogson and ask him if his wife knew her?'

'No need. I called on Sara Baker.'

'How could she tell you whether Brenda Pogson knew her?'

'Evidently that Starkey dame's a bit of a flighty piece. She was divorced about six months ago, and married a chap called Michael Turner. Mrs Michael Turner appears on Pogson's list.'

Masters sighed with relief. 'Did you get her address?'

'From the phone book.'

'We'll see her this afternoon. Just you and I.'

Green grunted. 'Are we going for a drink? Or is there something else you're going to tell me?'

Masters stretched his legs. Green, sitting on the upright chair, lit a Kensitas. Masters said: 'Both. I want a drink as much as you, so I'll make it snappy. I had an idea about how a murderer might knock somebody out without bruising them. Judo.'

'Why didn't I think of that?'

Masters told him of the demonstration.

'So it's a local bloke who knows judo. That cuts the numbers down a bit,' said Green.

'Considerably. Shall we have that drink now?'

*

Garner waited in the car outside. Masters and Green walked up the path to the house, which stood, end on, to Alexander Avenue. It was large, with two bays to the front, overlooking a narrow rose garden. As they stood by the front door they could see extensive lawns and flower beds beyond the house. Green said: 'For the second mate of a Finstoft drifter, she's done pretty well for herself. The rates alone on this place would make my pay look sick.'

Masters rang the bell.

Deadly Pattern

Mrs Turner herself answered. Master knew as soon as he saw her that she was the type Green liked. On the plumpish side. By no means fat, but, as Green had often expressed it, she filled her stockings well, which was only another way of saying that she had a good leg, shown off to advantage by the classic court shoes she wore, the thin, medium heels of which emphasized the slimness of the ankle and tautened the calves into an erotic firmness. She was dressed well. The navy-blue skirt, well cut, gave just a hint of roundness to her stomach. Not enough to require artificial hold-ins, but sufficient to give a suggestion of homeliness and warmth to the figure. Under the jacket of her suit her bosom, slightly too large, was provocative in a pale blue sweater. The thin gold chain round her neck hung over the protuberance and dangled like a climber's rope over an overhang. She was still dark-haired, and Masters could recognize the face from the picture of the Mary Starkey of a quarter of a century before. Plumper now, it was still impish and full of fun. But despite the careful make-up, there was something wrong. It took Masters a second or two to realize it was her eyes. Instead of being alight and mischievous, they were now wary and questioning. The eyes of a person bewildered and unsure.

'Mrs Turner?'

'Yes?'

'My name is Masters. I'm a police detective.'

'The one who's come to investigate the beach-hut murders?'

'That's me. May we come in and talk to you?'

'Talk to me? What about?' She was obviously puzzled. Masters guessed that it was not the fact that they wished to interview her that was causing her concern, but the fact that they had managed to pick her out for questioning. She was, he thought, wondering what they knew that had led them to her. It helped him. It gave him the unknown card, which was always so useful in interviews of this kind where probably the conversation might not be of material fact but simply an elicitation of opinion or an awakening of old memories.

'About the old days, mostly,' said Masters in a kindly voice. 'We should appreciate your co-operation.'

She held the door open wide. 'Come in, please. Will it take long? I was going shopping.'

Masters stepped in, followed by Green. It was a family home. Though scrupulously clean, it was friendly, with just a hint of untidiness to suggest that happy-go-lucky people lived there. The hall was square, and large enough to take several pieces of furniture, on all of which were odd-man-out articles. On a rosewood chair with mother-of-pearl inlay and pale pink upholstery was a riding crop and one small, yellow string glove. In the umbrella stand was a broken mashie, and on the bottom step of the lovely curving staircase a heap of freshly laundered linen which Masters guessed was waiting to be carried upstairs to an airing cupboard. Under the chandelier was a mobile, obviously the work of a child who had misjudged the balance, so that it hung lop-sided and motionless. But the chandelier itself was the sort that would have graced an embassy.

Mary Turner showed them into a sitting room on the left, at the back of the house. It had three windows, one on either side of the fireplace overlooking the garden, and a third looking out onto another small enclosure with a central pond and fountain. The carpets and curtains were good. They caressed Masters as he followed Mrs Turner in. The armchairs were the enveloping kind, big enough even for Masters, and upholstered in very pale grey and soft pink stripes separated by a gold thread.

They sat down. Mary Turner said: 'When you say you want to talk about the old days, what do you mean?'

'I think perhaps it will become clearer as we go along.'

She sat with her legs and feet together, her elbows on the chair arms, hands linked, her body slightly forward. Masters couldn't decide whether her attitude denoted expectancy or despair.

Masters said: 'How long have you been married—to Mr Turner?'

'Five months.'

'You married as soon as your divorce from Mr Tring became absolute?'

'Yes.'

'Who got that divorce? You or your previous husband?'

'I did.'

'Did you, during the case, ask for discretion to be exercised by the court in respect of your own adultery?'

She said, calmly: 'As a matter of fact, I did. But what has my divorce to do with the murders you are investigating?'

Green, too, was looking puzzled. This was not the line he had expected Masters to take. Still, Green thought, Masters always was devious, darting off down side-channels that a cop brought up to reverence the value of routine investigation would avoid like the plague.

'That's all I want to ask about that, Mrs Turner.'

'Maybe it is. But why ask any of it? Five women are killed and you suddenly appear on my doorstep and start asking questions like that. It doesn't make sense.'

Masters said quietly: 'It does—to me, Mrs Turner. And my advice to you is to stop being frightened. The danger's over.'

'Frightened?'

'Yes. You're covering up very well, but the worry has been there for some time now. How long? Six or seven weeks?'

She laughed. Rather too short and too shrill a laugh to be convincing. She said: 'What have I to be frightened of?'

'Murder.'

There was pause.

Masters went on: 'Was he queer as a schoolboy?'

She said 'Yes' and then bit her lip, as if to recall the slip.

'Right. Let's go on from there, shall we? You knew all the five murdered women?'

'How did you know that?'

'Please, Mrs Turner. It was simply a matter of finding out which people each one knew. You figured on all five lists.'

'I can't have done. I've not spoken to some of them for years.'

'So I guessed. You were friends as schoolgirls and then drifted apart. Was that it?'

She nodded.

'Tell me about it.'

She curled her legs up under her in the seat of the chair. 'When we were kids—about the fifth form, we used to go around in a bit of a gang. Not like the Mods and Rockers on scooters. We did ride bikes along the Prom, but we never caused any trouble. We played tennis together, and went in the ninepennies at the cinema and . . . oh, lots of things.'

'All girls?'

'Six of us.'

'The five who died and you?'

She nodded.

'What about boys?'

'That's what we did it for, I suppose. We were always meeting the sixth formers from the boys' grammar school. We used to congregate. Lord, how we used to play them up. We were real little devils, but when I look back on it, I can't remember us doing very much but talk in a crowd on the

Prom, or go to the bathing pool together, or something like that. When the boys were playing cricket matches we went and cheered. You know the sort of thing.'

'I think so.'

'We didn't take our relationships with boys quite as seriously as girls do these days. We weren't courting, you know. At sixteen these days they're frightened of being left on the shelf. In my days we wore summer frocks and blazers, bare legs and girls' shoes. We none of us had any money except a few bob pocket money. The boys were mostly expecting to go to university, and they didn't work in holidays like students do now. I expect that's why we congregated. We hadn't much else to do. But we enjoyed ourselves, I seem to remember.'

Masters gave her free rein. Let her gabble on to get it all out of her system. He said: 'The other five and you were in one particular gang.'

'We came from both Finstoft *and* Hawksfleet. It's funny how people drift together. But some of those girls were pretty. Really pretty. These days their looks alone would have got them somewhere. I was the exception that proved the rule. I wasn't bad looking in an impish sort of way, but I couldn't hold a candle to Joanna and Barbara, and you've only got to see Sara Baker to know what her mother was like.'

'We've seen her. She's a striking girl. Now let's talk about the boys.'

'Well, as I told you, they were sixth formers from Finstoft grammar school. You know, it was a funny thing. That school was—and still is—a maintained school . . .'

'What's that?' Green said.

'People paid for their children to go, except for about half a dozen scholarship boys each year who got free places.'

Green grunted. He sounded displeased. Mary Turner said: 'You don't approve? Well, perhaps you don't, but I'll tell you something about it. The boys whose parents paid—or most of them—would have passed the eleven plus. And the parents of the boys who got scholarships there would mostly have been willing to pay to get them in, because it's such a good school. Anyhow, at the time we're talking about, the sixth form was mostly made up of scholarship boys—the brilliant ones. The others usually left after taking their GCE, to go into their fathers' businesses.'

Masters said: 'So the fifth-form girls congregated with the sixth-form boys?'

'Well, it seemed natural in those days for a girl to be friendly with a boy a bit older than herself.'

'I can see that. But what about the sixth-form girls?'

'Oh, the ones that stayed on to the sixth were swots. Not the sort to want boy friends—or if they wanted them they didn't get them. All glasses and fringes and Eng. Lit., you know.'

Masters nodded. 'He was among the boys?'

She said, quietly: 'Yes.'

'Why? If he was so queer?'

'I think the boys had got used to him by then. He got a scholarship at eleven and went up the school with them. By the time they reached the sixth they accepted him as just somebody who'd always been there. He went about with them. He came from a poor home, but he was clever and his parents kept him very neat and clean.'

'But when he went along with his friends to join the girls?'

'Girls are little cats. They sense these differences. At least they do round here.'

'They snubbed him?'

'Well, I don't know about snubbed. He was always so serious. I know some of the girls—all of them, in fact—felt he was presuming on the friendship. As I say he was serious, and tried to get each one of us off on our own in turn.'

'And the girls wouldn't go with him?'

'That wasn't the way we normally did things.'

'Come now, Mrs Turner,' said Masters. 'It's not so very long ago. Even in those days youngsters used to pair off some of the time.'

'Well, yes, I suppose so.'

'I think you went out alone with him, didn't you?'

'Yes, I did. But it was funny. I think I was the only one of the six of us he didn't want. I told you the others were very pretty.'

'I think your kindness in those days saved your life recently.'

She sat up, startled. 'What?'

'I think you alone out of the six girls are alive today because you didn't snub him.'

'Oh, no.'

'Oh, yes. In spite of his queerness and poor home, you went out with him. The others turned him down. Why, do you think? Because he was a little odd? Or because of his social standing?'

She said slowly: 'Well, we were dreadful snobs, I remember.'

'They. Not you.'

'I thought he was rather a pet.'

'Good for you. What happened? All you girls left school?'

'The usual. As soon as we were out in the world mums and dads started match-making. One or two of the girls were married almost before they could get out of their gym knickers.'

'Not to the boys they had known.'

'No. To men five or six years older. Already established in family businesses. It really was sick-making. Beds ready made for virgins to be manœuvred into by their own parents, instead of being left to make their own.'

'Is that what happened in your case?'

She coloured slightly. 'I told you I wasn't quite as pretty as the rest of them and I was a young rip.'

'I approve of that. At least you're alive and . . .' He looked around him. '. . . not doing too badly, I'd have thought.'

She smiled for the first time. 'I'm a happy woman. Always have been.'

'Until this last month or so?'

'Yes. It's been hell.'

'How did you know?'

'I guessed. It seemed so obvious.'

'You didn't go to the police?'

'How could I? I hadn't guessed by the time they *started* disappearing. It was after all five had gone that I began to think things out. I began to wonder about myself. I was the sixth. The last. But I'd no *evidence*. Then the bodies started to be found. What could I do?'

'Had he been in touch with you?'

She shook her head and shuddered.

'Then why did you think he was involved?'

'I saw him one day when I was out walking. I knew him but couldn't place him. It was only when I started to think back to those days that I remembered him. Then I knew. I just knew. That's all.' She was near to hysteria and tears.

And with that Masters had to be satisfied. He felt it was useless to press Mary Turner further. As she had said, she had no evidence to give him. Green was entirely lost. He rose from his chair in complete bewilderment as Masters stood over her and said: 'Don't worry any more. And don't talk about it to anyone, please.'

She looked up at him. 'Would you like some tea?'

'Thank you, no. But why don't you make yourself some. It'll do you a power of good. We can let ourselves out.'

As they walked away from the house, Green said: 'Who the hell have you been talking about?'

'You haven't guessed?'

'Guessed? All I could guess was that from your questions about her divorce you were trying to find out whether she'd been keeping her hand on her ha'penny or not.'

'Quite right. She took her hand off it when she was sixteen, I suspect. She's been taking it off at intervals ever since from the sound of things. And that, I believe, has saved her life.'

Green pondered on this in the car. Neither spoke as Garner drove them to the Estuary. When they arrived at the hotel, Green said: 'I could have done with that cup of tea she offered us.'

Masters said: 'Order some here. I've a phone call to make. Then I'll join you.'

'And tell me what all this is about, I hope. I'm as much in the dark as a black pig's bottom.'

Masters didn't answer. He went to the reception desk. 'Page my two sergeants, Hill and Brant, please. Ask them to report to the lounge.'

While this was being done, Masters went into the telephone booth in the foyer. He called Bullimore and after him, Swaine. When he came out again he said to the receptionist: 'When phone calls are made in the hotel, how are they booked?'

'How d'you mean?'

'With S.T.D. you have to know how long and where to. How do you keep a check?'

The girl was unhelpful. 'Don't ask me. I just get a chit from our exchange, and put it on the bill.'

'Where is the hotel exchange?'

Reluctantly she let him through to a small room behind the reception desk. A girl was sitting writing a letter with single earphone on and microphone unclipped and lying beside her.

The receptionist said: 'Rosie, here's Detective Masters wants to know how you charge.'

Rosie was pleased to see him. She coloured when she realized who he was. She said: 'My Dad asked me if I'd seen you. He'd read about you in the paper. He was ever so disappointed when I said I hadn't. But I never see anybody when I'm cooped up in here. It's like being in prison. I can hear people ask for numbers and things . . .'

'Things?'

'Half of them ask me for early morning tea and papers when they should ring straight through to reception. It clutters me up, sort of.'

Masters grinned at her, and perched on the small table where her handbag and writing pad were. He said to the receptionist: 'Thank you very much. I mustn't keep you from your work or the manager'll be gunning for me. I just want a minute or two's private chat with Rosie, here.'

The receptionist sniffed to indicate that she wasn't the one to stay where she wasn't wanted and left the exchange room, closing the door with unnecessary firmness behind her. Masters said: 'Now look here, Rosie, anything I say in here is confidential. If you utter a word outside—to anybody—there'll be trouble.'

Her face fell. 'My Dad . . .'

'Tell him I just came in out of interest to see how you work. Nothing more. Understand?'

'Yes.'

'It's the truth anyway. Now. If I ring from my room, how do you know what charge to make on my bill?'

'That's simple. I have the code-book which tells me how much for how long at that distance, and I time you on and off with these.' She pointed to a row of box-like stop-clocks. 'I just multiply the number of units by the price of each unit and make out a chit for each call.'

'Fine. How do you make out the chits?'

She stared, not understanding the question.

'From beginning to end. Come on, go through the drill. I pick up the phone in my room. What happens?'

'Well, either the light goes up or the buzzer sounds as well as the light. I'm on the buzzer now, because there aren't many calls in the afternoon at this time of year and so I'm not watching the board all the time. When we're busy I *am* watching all the time so I switch to the lights only, otherwise I wouldn't be able to hear myself think.'

'So you hear the buzzer and the light shows you which line. What then?'

'I put in the jack. Then I want the room number. If the caller doesn't give it, I ask for it.'

'And?'

'I put it on the chit.' She picked up a small pad of tear-off chits.

'Then you ask for the number you are to dial?'

'That's right.'

'Do you put it down, too?'

'I've got to, otherwise I wouldn't remember these all figure-codes. I jot it down.'

'Good. That's all I wanted to know. Now, what happens to the chits?'

'They go to reception for putting on the bills.'

'What happens to them after that?'

'They come back in here for the book-keepers. I don't have anything to do with them. They're just kept to make up the telephone account which goes into the balance sheet. I think. But I don't know how they do it. Add them up, I suppose.'

'I think I know. The hotel doesn't want the money it takes in for phone calls to be charged as income for tax purposes, so they have to prove that it is money collected on behalf of the G.P.O. They need your chits to support the claim. And now I need them. But I'll speak to the manager first, so that you'll be in the clear. Probably my sergeants will collect them shortly.'

Masters left Rosie and made his way to the lounge. The other three were waiting for him. He said: 'We can't talk here, so tea first, then my room.'

Chapter Seven

'I don't believe it. Not Tintern. He's harmless,' said Green.

Masters said: 'Nevertheless I'm right. Now here's what's got to be done. Brant, I want you to check his phone call chits. Get to know the phone numbers of each of the victims, and his room number, and go through all the exchange accounts with a fine toothcomb. Garner's coming back to help you. He knows nothing about it yet, so grab him when he comes. I've spoken to the manager who will give you the chits himself. Examine them in your own room. I don't want little Rosie and that receptionist to know more than's necessary.'

'Right, chief. Start now?'

'Please. Now, Hill, your job is Tintern himself. From the moment he arrives in the pub until he's arrested, I want him under your eye—unobtrusively. It's five o'clock now. He must be about due, so get down there and be ready.'

Green said, when he and Masters were alone: 'What about me?'

'I want you to go outside and phone the Yard. I want details of Tintern's car crash some months ago.'

'Is that all?'

'It may be hellish important. After that, wait for Bullimore and Swaine and join me in his room. I'm going to search it.'

'What for?'

'Those women wore gloves and had purses. None of them has been found.'

'And you think they'll be there?'

'No. I don't. But I've got to make sure.'

Green lit a Kensitas. 'I'll look forward to hearing how you know. It's the screwiest case I've been on in years.' He got up to go.

'It's the nastiest. And the sooner we wrap it up the better.'

Tintern's room was tidy. There were few possessions in the drawers. Masters went through them carefully and found nothing to help him. In a suitcase on top of the wardrobe he found nothing of interest except an electric soldering iron, flux and solder. Disappointed, in spite of not expecting to find anything of value to him, he stood in the centre of the room and filled his pipe. He smoked reflectively. He had finished one pipe and was packing another when Bullimore and Swaine, carrying his bag, arrived with Green.

'Green tells me it's Tintern. I hope to God you're right,' Bullimore said.

Masters said: 'I am.' He didn't elaborate, and this left Bullimore mentally stranded. He remained uncomfortably quiet for a moment or two and then said: 'Do you want me to arrest him here?'

'As you like. Take him to the station if you'd prefer it.'

'I *would* prefer it. I want to hear your evidence before I take in a man on a multiple murder rap.'

Masters smiled. 'Doubting Thomas.'

'Did you find anything here?' said Green.

Masters handed him the soldering iron. 'This.' Green inspected it. 'What the hell's this got to do with it?'

'It had me foxed for a time. But I think it's the last link in the chain. Or the next to last. Would you care to ask Brant if he and Garner have turned anything up?'

Green lit a Kensitas, and then remembering his manners offered one to Bullimore who refused it. Swaine took one, and as Green left the room, said: 'I know you haven't made a dog's breakfast of it. Can feel it in my bones. But I can't for the life of me see how you've done it. Dammit, man, I've been with you half the time you've been here and you haven't produced a tangible clue.'

'What about the fifth body?'

'Was that a clue?'

Masters nodded.

'Well, that was tangible enough. Stank to glory.'

The phone bell went.

Masters picked it up. Hill's voice said: 'He's here, but he's gone straight down for a drink.'

'Right. Watch him.' He turned back to the others. 'We've got at least fifteen minutes—probably half an hour.'

Bullimore said: 'In that case give us a rundown on the evidence.'

'We'd better sit if we can find room.' Masters remained standing. Bullimore took the armchair. Swaine perched on the case stand.

Masters said: 'From the outset we were convinced that this crime was carried out by a local man . . .'

'I told you so the first day,' said Bullimore. 'And now you're going into reverse. Tintern . . .'

Masters interrupted: '. . . is a native of Finstoft. Born here and lived here until he left school about the age of eighteen or nineteen. That's well over twenty years ago.'

'Are you sure? I mean, I don't know him.'

'Would you? After a gap of about a quarter of a century? An insignificant lad? What were you then? A constable? Sergeant perhaps?'

'Come to think of it, I wasn't even in Finstoft then. You get moved around in a County force, you know.'

'Before my time, too,' said Swaine.

Masters went on: 'I've waited to see if Garner would recognize him. But he hasn't. And if an old Tofter copper can't recognize one of his own kind, very few others would, either. However, I found one person who recognized him, but only after her mind had been jerked backwards over the years by your crop of murders. But let's get on, shall we?'

'Wait a moment. How did you find out Tintern was Finstoft born and bred?' Bullimore asked.

Masters turned to Swaine. 'When we were having a drink at lunchtime on Sunday, Garner used an expression I'd never heard before.'

'What was it?'

'"Pounding the clits". I guessed he meant walking over the dunes.'

'Lord, yes. Clits. I haven't heard it myself for years. You're quite right, of course. You won't hear anybody, anywhere, using that word except a real old Tofter and perhaps a Dane. You see, clit is Danish for dune. It was imported by the invaders and got left behind.'

'I didn't know the history of it, but I guessed it must be an old word peculiar to Finstoft,' said Masters.

'Not to Finstoft as a whole. Just to people born here of old Tofter families. Like Garner. I'd never use it myself. Apart from the fact that it wouldn't come natural, it smacks of a certain part of the internal anatomy of the female which, now I come to think about it, can be dune- or dome-shaped. And just imagine the impression I'd create if I went around talking about "pounding the clits". Old Bullimore here would run me in for indecent exposure or something.'

Bullimore said: 'What's Garner's lingo got to do with Tintern?'

'On Sunday evening, Tintern used the same word. "These gentlemen need a good stiff drink after climbing about over the clits all day." Hearing that particular—and unfamiliar—word again so soon caused it to stick in my mind. I'd already decided it must be a Finstoft word, but taken alone it didn't necessarily indicate that Tintern was a Tofter. He could have picked the word up anywhere—from the workmen at the church, for instance. But, as I said, it made me think. And I'd already asked myself why an architect as famous as Tintern should stay here in Finstoft for a couple of months to supervise a church restoration. I'd have expected him to come and go like any other busy man would.'

'You use everyday facts to make shackles. Honest you do,' said Bullimore.

What else he was about to say was interrupted by Green who came in full of excitement. He said: 'We've got one. He phoned the Osborn house on Sunday the twenty-sixth. You remember. Her son said Joanna took an unknown call on that afternoon.'

'That one alone will do for us. But if they can get others it'll help to substantiate,' said Masters.

Bullimore said: 'Now what's going on?'

'We're tracing Tintern's calls through the hotel exchange. We know he phoned the Osborns two days before Joanna disappeared. We'll probably get further confirmation that he was in touch with all these women.'

'You people frighten me,' said Swaine.

Masters said: 'What d'you expect? Footprints, fingerprints, bloodstains and blunt instruments?'

'Something of the sort, I suppose.'

'You'll not get them in this case. But to get on. You can take it from me, Tintern is a Tofter, and I visited the registrar to prove it. It cost me one and nine to have a look. I'll be putting it on the expenses sheet. My next problem was to discover how the murderer managed to strangle his victims without the traditional scratches showing on the neck. It took some thinking about, but once I was on to it, it was so obvious it made me want to cry. Judo.'

'Cripes. Is there a hold . . .?' said Swaine.

'A snatch, I think you'd call it. With crossed hands from the coat collar jarring nerves in the neck.'

'What nerves?' asked Bullimore.

Swaine said: 'If you want me to be specific, I'd have to look it up. But I can give you the general picture if you like.'

'I would like.'

'Well, there are two sorts of nerve fibre. Sensory and motor. Sensory for sensation, motor for movement. And at various parts of the body—particularly in the neck—these are bound together in great sheaths. One bundle for each side of the body and the opposite side of the brain. And what travels along nerves are impulses, caused by stimuli. These stimuli can be caused by electrical shock, heat or cold, chemicals or—as in this case—mechanical means. If the stimulus is strong enough at one certain point it raises the local excitatory state of the nerves to a critical value and a disturbance spreads at high velocity along the nerve. Now if this impulse is sharp enough to excite practically every nerve in the body all at once, you can imagine the brain's response. It passes out. And it stays out for some time, because these impulses are like a spark travelling along a trail of gunpowder—except that they travel about a hundred and twenty-five yards in a second—and they leave a trail of burnt out powder behind. No other spark can travel that way until the trail has been relaid. And this is exactly what nerves do. They regenerate themselves. When we're living and moving normally, we have relays of nerves. One takes over when another is played out and so we can have constant motion and sensation, with each nerve burning out, regenerating and coming into play again when necessary. But if a sharp flick stimulates every nerve at once, they're all burnt out at once, and the body's useless for a given length of time. Possibly only for seconds . . .'

'It was demonstrated on Sergeant Hill,' said Masters. 'He was out for only a short time.'

'But long enough for somebody to strangle him unhampered?'

'I think a strangler applying pressure would have kept him unconscious.'

'Then that explains that,' said Bullimore. 'But would Tintern know such a hold or snatch or whatever it is?'

'I have no absolute proof that he did. But he studied judo in Hawksfleet under a chap called Shen Ma Pang, in Acre Yard in Hawksfleet.'

'Did he, now?'

'Shen's a bit cagey. This particular snatch is not supposed to be taught and he says he didn't teach it to Tintern. However, he suggested Tintern could have seen it being demonstrated among judo experts. It's a point you'll have to clear up. Can you get the Hawksfleet people to lean on Shen to get the truth if the prosecution needs it? Personally I don't think it will be vital to the case, because whether their necks were scratched or not, the women died. But it might be useful circumstantially to point out that Tintern learned judo.'

'Leave it to me,' said Bullimore.

Masters went on. 'So I had a native Tofter who knew judo, staying for a remarkably long time here on a flimsy excuse. I hope by now you'll see I had good cause to suspect Tintern.'

Bullimore grunted.

'But it was Tintern's behaviour that clinched matters. We were all talking about a madman—a dangerous lunatic. I don't know much about neuroses and psychiatric disorders, so I borrowed the doc's little books. But before that, the doc had said that a neurosis could be triggered off by one severely shocking experience or it could appear gradually due to environmental pressures. With my mind firmly fixed on Tintern, I remembered that a few months ago he had come physically unscathed through a serious car accident on a motorway. But though he was unhurt, I seemed to remember somebody was killed.'

Green said: 'That's right. His wife and only child.'

There was silence for a moment.

Masters went on: 'I hadn't realized it was as personal as that. That's a shock big enough to send any man off his rocker. But to get back to doc's books. I came across our old friend dementia praecox. I say old friend, because that's the sort of name that, once heard, tends to stick in the mind, even if you don't know what it means. So, because it sounded familiar I read it carefully. I can now quote the definition given. It's this. "*Term for a large group of psychoses of psychogenic origin, often recognized during or shortly after adolescence but frequently in later maturity, characterized by disorientation, loss of contact with reality, splitting of the personality: schizophrenia.*" And it was that last word that did things for me. I turned to the schizophrenic symptoms and I read those up.'

'What did you get?' said Swaine.

'The first was symbolism in behaviour and speech. Now you'll remember that symbolism was another word we were bandying about, because the bodies were all laid out in the same way, hands and feet spreadeagled, all heads pointing east and so on. And there was the fifth body. I haven't explained to you how I came to find it. I will now.' He took from his inside pocket the large scale plan of the area, and spreading it in front of them described how he had come to realize that a perfect cross, pointing east, would be formed by a body buried where the two arms crossed. He went on: 'We found the fifth body as you know. But the really important part is that the book said schizophrenic symbolism was usually either religious or sexual. And this burial pattern screamed out that it was religious symbolism. And Tintern has devoted his life to restoring religious buildings. What is more, he is an architect and surveyor. Who but a trained man could lay out five bodies so exactly? It is only because Inspector Green has a working knowledge of artillery survey that we were able to make sense out of four bodies dotted about in an apparently aimless manner.'

Bullimore turned to Green. 'I'll see you don't lose by it. We have a merit award system here for bits of good work like that.'

'Thanks.'

Masters said: 'Some of the other manifestations of schizophrenia also applied to Tintern. One of them is that they see objects change shape and colour. Once when I was in the bar he pointed to a colourless bottle and told me it was red. At the time I thought it might be reflecting a red fairy-light, but now I know it wasn't. Then there was one of the most characteristic facets of the disease—disturbance of thinking. In the book it gave as an example a schizophrenic who had translated the old saying "a stitch in time saves nine" into "I must sew nine buttons on my coat". All four of us heard on Sunday morning, at breakfast time, a waiter say to Tintern, "You get that down pretty nippy like and you'll find you've made up for lost time." Tintern's reply was, "I've lost my time maid."'

Swaine said: 'Good lord. Anything else?'

'There's oceans of it. According to your book schizos often answer questions by using the same words as the question is asked in. Green will bear me out that Tintern nearly always repeated a questioner's words—like one of those inept interviewees on television.'

'That's right. Like a parrot,' said Green.

Masters went on: 'And his shirt. He wore one with a smudged collar all Saturday and Sunday. The book says they don't change dirty garments for weeks, sometimes. And the row about his change in the bar. Shirl says it has often happened. But for an example of unpredictable variability what do you think of a man who can't work out change for a pound note, but who can play chess and bridge extremely well?'

'It's conclusive enough,' said Swaine.

'There is more. Examples of social withdrawal—when he wouldn't speak to us one day and was standing us drinks the next. Persecution mania—he complained the chambermaids wouldn't let him use the nearest lavatory. And, I believe, one other very conclusive example. He must have realized that something was wrong with him, and he made desperate attempts to regain control in what the book says is the typical way—by trying to stick to a rigid timetable, diet, etcetera. He was cross because he wasn't wakened on time, and he wouldn't eat a decent breakfast. The signs are numerous, and though they may not make good evidence in court they certainly bolster up the reason for his arrest.'

Bullimore said: 'I agree. But you haven't so far given us any reason for the killings, or any reason for his choice of victims. And without those we'll get nowhere.'

Masters grinned as he lit his pipe. He said to Bullimore: 'You gave me the hint that first day when you spoke about the social strata in Finstoft and Hawksfleet. Why break the noses of dead women?'

'To put them out of joint, like as not,' said Green.

'Right. That's what occurred to me. Noses out of joint—socially. The reaction of an unbalanced mind to real or imaginary social slights in the past. You know, the obvious step in multiple crime is to look for common factors, common contacts or some other means of connecting them. This time I felt sure there must be a common contact—probably several. But we satisfied ourselves with one. A Mrs Mary Turner. She was known to all these women many years ago. She was friendly with them all when they were senior schoolgirls. She's given us an account of what went on between that group of girls and their boy friends at that time.'

'Was Tintern one of them?' Swaine asked.

'Yes. But he was odd man out. The girls fought shy of being alone with him. They tolerated him in the group, but refused single dates with him. I believe he thought at the time that they shunned him because he came of a working-class family. That's the impression a poor lad would get in this area at that time, isn't it, Super?'

'As like as not.'

'Personally, I think he wasn't snubbed by these girls—socially, I mean. I believe that even at the age of eighteen he was beginning to show some of the signs of his schizophrenia, and that frightened them off from being alone with him. Remember the definition says that the disease is often recognized during or shortly after adolescence. And one of the main symptoms is sensitivity—more developed than in the normal person. A hypersensitivity which causes them to over-respond to any stimulus. I think he over-responded to the attraction these girls had for him. He grew fanatically entangled in his emotions, and when they wouldn't play, he was so oversensitive to their response that he misinterpreted it and it became a mania.'

Swaine said: 'That's supposition, surely.'

'Maybe. But Mary Turner will tell you that out of the six girls involved she was the only one who did accommodate him, and she's the only one who's still alive.'

'Accommodate him?'

'She was a lively young imp. She's been married twice and divorced once. I go no further than that. But she's not a frigid type, and whatever she got up to with Tintern was powerful enough to save her life more than twenty years later. I think Inspector Green was right when he described her as a girl who hadn't always kept her hand on her ha'penny.'

Swaine laughed and said: 'I must remember that one.'

Bullimore said: 'So he was shunned because he was odd, due to the beginnings of schizophrenia. Because of sexual emotions he mistook the girls' standoffishness for snobbery. That stayed with him, rankling in his subconscious, until the death of his wife and child triggered off fully developed schizophrenia. Then the hurt in his mind came to the surface and he took his revenge.'

'I can't give a specific answer as to whether he accepted the job of restoring the local church with a view to coming here for revenge or whether, having accepted the job the old environment put revenge into his mind . . .'

'Neither can anybody else. And the question is academic. He's unfit to plead,' said Swaine.

'I'm afraid he is. But to go back to which came first—the job or thoughts of revenge. I've said I can't be dogmatic about the time when this crazy decision came to him, and the doctor says nobody can be definite, but I believe he came here with the express intention of murdering these women.'

'Mind reading? Or are there some facts to base your assumption on?' Bullimore asked.

'Call it, rather, lack of facts.'

Dr Swaine laughed. 'By the Lord Harry, I enjoy being around when you're on the job. Now you can make deductions from lack of facts; and

I'll put ten to one on your being right without hearing what you've got to say.'

Masters grinned. 'It's what *you'd* call differential diagnosis. It pertains to the differences between what happened to me when I came to Finstoft and what happened to Tintern.'

Swaine said: 'I should have known better than lend you that medical dictionary. I knew instinctively I'd have it cast in my teeth before very long.'

'Give over, you two. What's the griff?' said Bullimore.

'When I arrived the local paper wrote me up, as I imagine it does all notorious visitors to the area, given the chance. Who told them I was here?'

Bullimore, rather shamefacedly, said: 'I did. Those reporters were living at the station. I gave them your arrival to keep them happy for a bit—and off my back.'

'I don't blame you. But as nobody here seems to know that Tintern is a Tofter, I assume he never got a write-up in the local rag.'

'I never saw one.'

'Nor me,' said Swaine.

'Which would seem to indicate there wasn't a mention of him, although he's a pretty famous chap in his own field. If they'd got to know about him, the editor would have soon dug out the fact that Tintern was born here and have splurged about a local boy making good, wouldn't he?'

'Without a doubt.'

'So everybody would have known he was a Tofter. And that fact alone would've spoiled his plans. My belief is that the vicar of the church he's been rebuilding would've made a point of mentioning his presence to reporters, unless he'd been specifically asked not to do so.'

'By Tintern himself?'

Masters nodded. 'You can check up with the vicar, but I imagine when he first arrived, Tintern explained that he'd just lost his wife and child and he'd come here for a rest as much as anything else. He would prefer no publicity. And the vicar would be the first to agree to so reasonable a request. That's what must have happened, because though he's been away from here for a quarter of a century, there must still be some people round here who would remember him—his school contemporaries, if nobody else. And had they known he'd returned to Finstoft, one or other of them would have been bound to make some remark about it, and the word would have spread.'

'But you think Tintern was cunning enough to foresee the need for secrecy and provide for it?' said Swaine.

'I do. But the proof must be sought from the vicar. The Super will, no doubt, do that tomorrow.'

Bullimore said: 'You bet I will.'

The door opened and Brant came in. He said: 'That girl Rosie didn't give the numbers for all the local calls. But beside Osborn, we know he contacted Baker.'

'Thank you. Find Hill and try to let us know what Tintern's up to and whether he shows any signs of leaving the bar.' Brant turned to the door. As he did so, it burst open, and Tintern stumbled in. For a moment he stood staring at them, and then turned to flee. Hill was blocking the way. Bullimore said: 'Come in, Mr Tintern, we want to talk to you.'

As he stepped forward, Tintern held out an arm as if to hold him off, and then, with a little moan, started to crumple at the knees. Hill stepped forward and caught him. Lowered him to the ground. Swaine said: 'On to the bed with him.'

They lifted him gently. Swaine loosened his collar and examined him. Even used a stethoscope and took his blood pressure with the sphygmomanometer he carried in his bag. The others stood around, watching and waiting.

Swaine finally straightened up. 'Acute schizophrenic breakdown. I don't know much about psychiatry, but I do know the medical symptoms. Dilated pupils, moist palms, moderate tachycardia, and a systolic blood pressure of about fifteen mils above what it should be.'

'Is he in any danger?' Bullimore asked.

'No. We shall need an ambulance for him, but I think a good night's rest in hospital and a dose of largactil will see him as right as he ever will be in the morning.'

'But tachycardia—that's heart trouble, isn't it? And high blood pressure . . .'

'Doesn't amount to anything. Tachycardia only means excessive rapidity of the heart beat. It's due to what I believe is known in these cases as sympathetic excitement.'

Bullimore rang for an ambulance. Swaine stood by his patient. Green said to Masters: 'Why did a chap like that learn judo?'

'I don't know. But my guess is he thought it would even things up. It's a well-known fantasy with some of these characters that they like to imagine themselves taking on all comers. And a chap with an asthenic build like Tintern's . . .'

'A what?'

'Sorry. I got it out of the doc's book. Asthenic. It means weak, willowy, nervy-looking. It's the classic build for a schizo. A chap like him couldn't take on anybody without the help of judo or a machine-gun. So I suppose he learned judo. But as I say it's only a guess.'

'Sounds good enough to me,' said Hill.

Bullimore came across. 'It's on its way. With an escort. He'll be kept under surveillance.'

'Fine.'

'You've done a damn fine job for us, Chief Inspector.'

'I'm pleased we got it cleared up so quickly. Now your women needn't be frightened of the dark any more. And I'll let you have my report by lunchtime tomorrow.'

Bullimore said: 'There are a couple of things you haven't explained. First, the soldering iron.'

Masters grinned. 'This is a guess. And I'll leave you to prove or disprove it. It concerns the belongings of these women which we haven't found despite our searches. My belief, based on my knowledge of Tintern's mind and finding that soldering iron, is that he put them all in a metal canister, soldered the lid on, and put them into the church wall. In the cement they're pumping in.'

'And you expect me to find it? He could have done it weeks ago.'

'I don't think so. Look at it this way. Suppose you were an architect accustomed to rebuilding old churches. One of the usual practices on these occasions is to immure—in a container—certain present-day articles which will prove of interest in hundreds of years' time, when it comes to be discovered. Almost without exception, one of the articles so buried is a current newspaper. Right, so far?'

Bullimore nodded. 'If you say so.'

'Now you are not only an architect involved in these practices, but you are also a murderer with certain small articles belonging to your victims that you want to dispose of. You are running liquid cement into cavity walls. What better hiding-place for these articles is likely to occur to you, than to bury them in the cement?'

'None. It's a damn good idea. Couldn't be bettered.'

'Right. But you are not a mason or a workman. If you are seen stuffing gloves and purses into the cement, somebody might ask questions. So you think again. Nobody will ask questions if you follow the usual practice and bury a canister. You know where to obtain one, because you've used them before. But this time, because the contents will be incriminating, you don't get a workman to solder the lid on. You buy yourself a soldering iron and you do it yourself in the privacy of your own bedroom. And because you usually include a newspaper, what better idea could you get than to wait for, and include, a newspaper that contains an account of the murders to which the other articles are vital clues? Think of the sensation that might cause in a couple of hundred years' time. And if, in addition, you're a schizophrenic, think how such future notoriety will feed your delusions of grandeur. Besides, burial of these articles in a church wall will be a splendid act of religious symbolism. So that's what you do. When did the story break in the newspapers?'

'Last Wednesday.'

'Say Tintern did his soldering on Wednesday evening, he would have his canister ready for burial on Thursday. Go and ask the foreman at the church where it was put.'

'Would the foreman know?'

'I think so. He'd be able to do it openly, you know. It's a custom, so nobody would suspect anything.'

'Right. I'll do that. And now, last of all, how did he persuade them to meet him?'

'Another guess—because we shall never know. But these women were living humdrum lives. Not one of them was really doing anything. Playing at decorating hats or indulging in social work to ease the boredom. You'd know about that better than I would. So put yourself in their place. One day, out of the blue, comes a call from a man whom you had known in far-off, more carefree days—a man whom you'd not been too keen on at the time, but who, in spite of that, had made such a success of his life that he was now a national figure in his own field. And when he revisits the area after many years, one of the first things he does is ring you up. Flattering? Of course it is. Already you are viewing the past with rose-coloured spectacles. The man you didn't think much of has seemed for a long time to be not so bad after all. Perhaps you misjudged him. After all, he's now famous: accepted. Who are you to steer clear of him when he singles you out for attention? Remembers you after so many years? You don't snub him now. You welcome the call. He's still a bit odd. But all geniuses are odd, aren't they? And what does his oddness amount to? Very little. All he's asking is that you should come out for a drink and a chat about the old days *without telling your husband.* He says—with a laugh—that he's a bit scared of jealous husbands. A joke, perhaps, but why not humour him? After all it will be a bit of fun—a bit of a daring change—to go out secretly with an old flame. So why not? Why not go out and meet him? Have a nostalgic evening with no husband or children or anybody being the wiser? Why not meet him?'

Bullimore said: 'By crikey, you've an imagination. And you make it sound as if you were there.'

*

Tintern was taken away. Swaine said: 'He's going to hospital, so I'm not going with him. But I could do with a drink. What about it?'

They accompanied him to the Sundowner.

Shirl said: 'I hear Mr Tintern's been took bad.'

Swaine said: 'He's not a strong man. I sent him to hospital.'

'I *am* sorry to hear that. The usual for you gentlemen?'

Masters thought this was typical. A life and death crisis dismissed in half a dozen words. He wondered if Shirl would understand that an argument about change at her bar had helped to uncover a mass murderer. He supposed it was better that she shouldn't.

Swaine raised his glass: 'Here's to the health of your blood.'

'And here's to your bloody good health,' said Green.

*

Masters was packing his suitcase at ten o'clock the next morning. The phone rang. It was Bullimore. 'You were right. A flat copper box. One end soldered on amateurishly. Stuffed full of you-know-what. And the vicar says you were right about the publicity.'

Masters said slowly: 'Fine. That wraps it up for you very nicely.'

He put the phone down and returned to his packing.

Made in the USA
Columbia, SC
27 February 2021